THE
PEREGRINATIONS
OF THE
PERPLEXING
NASRUDIN

TAHIR SHAH

THE
PEREGRINATIONS
OF THE
PERPLEXING
NASRUDIN

TAHIR SHAH

MMXXI

Secretum Mundi Publishing Ltd
Kemp House
City Road
London
EC1V 2NX
United Kingdom

www.secretum-mundi.com
info@secretum-mundi.com

First published by Secretum Mundi Publishing Ltd, 2021
VERSION 03062021

THE PEREGRINATIONS OF THE PERPLEXING NASRUDIN

© TAHIR SHAH

Tahir Shah asserts the right to be identified as the Author of the Work
in accordance with the Copyright, Designs and Patents Act 1988.
A CIP catalogue record for this title is available from the British Library.

Visit the author's website at:

Tahirshah.com

ISBN 978-1-912383-79-5

For Pat and David

CONTENTS

OAKLAND
CALIFORNIA

Reverse Thinking

Moving at high speed, Nasrudin hurried backwards into a shop in Jack London Square.

After rushing from left to right, he bustled out again – all of it in reverse.

Then, still going backwards, he hurried across the main street, down steps leading to the car park, climbed into his car, and reversed it out into the traffic.

A policeman on patrol stopped him and demanded to know what was going on.

'Hello officer,' the wise fool replied courteously, 'I've forgotten the address of my friend who lives near here.'

The police officer glared.

'That doesn't explain why you're driving backwards so dangerously!'

'Oh, but it does, sir,' Nasrudin explained. 'You see, I'm simply going back until I reach the last time I was there.'

EASTER ISLAND

CHILE

Wrong Donkey

Nasrudin had arrived on Easter Island with his donkey on the pretext of looking for rare fossils.

Right from the start he had other intentions.

While all the islanders and the other tourists were asleep, he took a thick rope, and rode his donkey out to one of the largest of the stone heads for which the island is famed.

Having tied one end of the rope to the donkey, he fastened the other around the stone head.

Irritated at having to work in the middle of night, the donkey brayed long and hard.

Within a few minutes a security guard was on the scene.

Nasrudin was charged and appeared in court the next day.

The judge took a very dim view of his behaviour.

'It seems that you chose the wrong thing to drag behind that animal of yours!' he boomed.

'On the contrary,' the wise fool answered. 'I didn't choose the wrong thing to drag… I chose the wrong donkey with which to drag it!'

LONDON
ENGLAND

Serial Giver Upper

Nasrudin was a serial giver upper.

As soon as he started anything, he gave it up.

One by one, he worked his way through every evening class held in London's metropolitan area and, one by one, he gave up.

A friend asked about his condition.

'I don't know why I have it,' he said miserably. 'The only thing I haven't given up is giving up!'

FRANKFURT
GERMANY

Humour vs. Fashion

Nasrudin had a pet boa constrictor named Bertie, which he took everywhere.

Rather than put the creature in a cage, he would wear him around his neck, amazing some, and terrifying others.

One day, while travelling through Europe, the wise fool was arrested for transporting an unlicenced reptile into Germany.

Nasrudin couldn't understand what all the fuss was about.

'You're not hearing what I am saying,' he said to the customs agent. 'This isn't an unlicenced reptile. It's Bertie.'

'If your little friend Bertie isn't a reptile, then what is he?' the official asked gruffly.

'He's part of my attire.'

'I warn you,' the officer scoffed, 'for this job I am trained to have no sense of humour.'

Nasrudin rolled his eyes.

'I'm not asking for a sense of humour, officer,' he replied caustically. 'What I'm asking for is a sense of fashion!'

BANGKOK
THAILAND

The Foibles of Man

n a journey through the Far East, Nasrudin bumped into an old school friend, who had moved to Bangkok and reinvented himself as a crypto-currency trader – making himself a fortune in the process.

The wealth had led to fame and, in turn, the fame had brought adulation from thousands of young investors who regarded him as the Crypto-Currency King.

Meeting such an old friend as Nasrudin, the trader was at ease for once.

'What a strange thing this is,' he exclaimed.

'What is?'

The trader sighed.

'I've spent a lifetime trying to make a name for myself, but without any luck. As you know, I've failed in almost everything I ever set out to do. Then I bought and sold something that, technically speaking, doesn't exist, and was catapulted to stardom.'

Nasrudin looked at the Crypto-Currency King sideways.

'If I were you I'd keep such thoughts to yourself,' he replied, 'and give thanks to the foibles of man.'

EYJAFJALLAJÖKULL
ICELAND

Beginner's Luck

Nasrudin was spotted climbing the infamous volcano on a lone mission to rappel down into the interior, with nothing more than a rope.

Fearful that yet another foreigner was about to die at the hands of the active volcano, the Icelandic authorities dispatched a team of seasoned volcanologists to bring him back.

Having scaled the volcano, the experts reached the crater and peered down into the interior, from which sulphurous gas was spewing.

'Climb up at once!' the team leader barked through a megaphone.

'You won't be able to breathe!' a second member of the team bellowed.

'The heat will char you to a crisp!' warned a third.

'What safety equipment do you have with you?!' the leader yelled.

There was no reply – not at first, anyway.

After a minute or two, a faint voice called up from far below.

'My safety equipment consists of a pouch containing prayers and a rucksack full of beginner's luck!'

LOS ANGELES
CALIFORNIA

Trendsetting Fool

Nasrudin went to a cosmetic surgeon in Beverly Hills and announced that he was about to give the physician the biggest job of his life.

'When you're done with me,' he beamed, 'you'll be able to retire and buy a big yacht!'

'What exactly do you have in mind, sir?' the surgeon asked. 'I can't see anything that needs changing.'

'Well,' the wise fool responded, 'I'd like my eyes swapped around with my ears, and my mouth put up nice and high on my forehead. Then, I'd like my nose shifted down onto my chin… and my chin moved round to the back of my head.'

In his line of work, the physician met a lot of deranged patients, but Nasrudin took the prize for the nuttiest of all.

'If I were you,' the surgeon intoned gently, 'I would get on with your life and stop trying to play God.'

'It's not that I want to play God,' he replied, 'but rather that I'm a trendsetter in the Land of the Fools.'

'And what does that mean, exactly?'

'That I'm hoping to stir things up and kick off a new trend!'

BISHKEK
KYRGYZSTAN

The Premonition

n the second day after his arrival in the Kyrgyz capital, Nasrudin awoke in the night with a start.

The dream he'd been having had ended in death…

The death of the president, whose face was everywhere – from oversized portraits on public buildings to the giant flags flapping on the wide boulevards.

Terrified out of his wits, the wise fool knew one thing, and one thing alone – that he had to warn the president that he was about to be assassinated.

Still wearing his pyjamas, Nasrudin went out to the street, hailed a taxi, and demanded to be taken to the presidential palace.

'Do you have an appointment?' the driver whispered, as he zigzagged through the empty streets.

'No, I don't. But the president will definitely want to see me.'

The driver looked at the passenger in the rear-view mirror, taking in his pyjamas.

'Are you a dignitary of some kind?' he asked in bewilderment.

The wise fool shook his head.

'No, but I've had a premonition!'

'What kind?'

'That the president of the republic is about to be strangled to death!'

At that moment, the taxi arrived at the gates of the Ala Archa State Residence, where the head of state lived.

Nasrudin climbed down, ran to the gates, and pleaded to be let in.

'I've had a premonition!' he wailed. 'It's a matter of life and death!'

Raising their weapons, the guards ordered for the outcry to cease, but Nasrudin wouldn't pipe down. Rather, he grew far louder.

'If you don't let me pass on this information, I'll wake the entire city!' he yelled.

Even though the hour was late, it just so happened that the president was at his desk. Hearing a disturbance outside, he went to the window, peered out, and saw what looked and sounded like a foreigner in his pyjamas.

Intrigued, the head of state instructed a guard to bring the man inside.

Ten minutes later, the wise fool was brought into the president's private study.

Without delay, details of the premonition were passed on:

'I saw a man of about my height striding up behind you and strangling you with both hands, like this…'

Nasrudin acted it out, as though he were throttling a man to death.

The president seemed alarmed.

'Have you had premonitions before?'

'Well, not actual premonitions with importance like this,' Nasrudin replied, 'but I did once dream that a goat with two heads would be born in the next village.'

'And was it?'

'Yes!'

The chief of security was called.

'Double the guard,' the president said, 'and make sure that our friend…'

'*Nasrudin*, my name's Nasrudin.'

'Make sure that our friend, Mr. Nasrudin, is given accommodation here in the palace. Time will tell if his premonition comes true. And if an attack happens, I expect your team to deal with it long before the attacker gets to my neck!'

'At your service, Excellence!' the head of security cried, saluting.

Accordingly, the presidential guard was doubled, and the wise fool was taken to a sumptuous guest room where, having arrived in his pyjamas, he climbed into a massive four-poster bed.

In the morning, Nasrudin was given a delicious breakfast. He asked the chief of police whether there had been any sight of an assassin.

'No, but we have quadrupled the guard,' was the answer.

With the president very busy with matters of state, and the guard preoccupied with ensuring the leader was kept alive, everyone forgot about the wise fool.

As a presidential guest, Nasrudin was given anything he wished, from his own bevy of guards to use of the presidential yacht.

A week passed.

Then another.

One morning, the president remembered the incident, in which a foreigner had turned up in his pyjamas, claiming to have had a premonition.

'Whatever happened to that odd fellow, the one in his pyjamas?' he asked the head of security at a routine briefing later that morning.

'He is still in the palace, Your Excellence.'

The president touched a hand to his chin.

'Well, I have not been strangled as he said I would, so I think it's time for him to go on his way.'

'Of course, Excellence,' said the chief of security.

'Wait a minute,' the president faltered. 'Before he leaves, I'd like to see him again.'

That afternoon, Nasrudin was brought into the study once again. In his hand was a bag containing soap, shampoo, shower caps, and all kinds of other mementoes he'd pilfered during his stay.

The president greeted the guest, still wearing pyjamas.

'Well, as you see, no attempt has been made on my life,' he said.

'Not yet, Mr. President,' Nasrudin intoned darkly.

'What do you mean "*Not yet*"?'

'You see, the details of my premonition were unclear. There's no way of knowing when the attack is to take place.'

The president sighed.

'Tell me exactly what you remember from your dream.'

Closing his eyes, Nasrudin thought hard.

'I can see you sitting behind your desk, exactly where you are now,' he said. 'There's a man standing behind you. He's got a chain in his hands, the kind you would use if you were going to strangle someone.'

'Tell me more! What does he look like?'

Again, Nasrudin closed his eyes and focused.

'Oh! Gosh! How strange!' Nasrudin blurted.

'What is? What's strange?'

'The man standing behind you with the chain… ready to strangle you… I can see his face very clearly.'

'Is it a face you know?'

'Yes!' Nasrudin exclaimed jubilantly. 'I know it very, very well.'

'Whose face is it?'

'It's my own!'

The president of the republic clapped his hands together.

'Guards! Throw this man out at once!'

PYEONGCHANG
SOUTH KOREA

Donkey Bobsleigh

aving challenged the rules of the Olympic Committee, Nasrudin entered himself in his national one-man bobsleigh team.

Nowhere in the rule book did it say what material a sleigh had to be made from, or whether it could be alive. So, having starved his poor donkey for several weeks so that she reached the required weight, he was ready for the race.

Having led the animal to the top of the piste, he clambered on, and off they went.

Hurtling through one zigzag bend after the next, the wise fool and his ever-faithful steed reached breakneck speeds and zipped across the finish line much faster than anyone else.

Interviewed after the award ceremony, Nasrudin was asked how he had managed to go so fast.

'Unlike the competition,' he explained, 'my model of donkey-bobsleigh doesn't have brakes. So, even if we had wanted to slow down, we couldn't.'

'Weren't you worried that other competitors would lampoon you for being different?'

The wise fool grinned at the journalist's question.

'Who in his right mind would want to be like everyone else?' he asked. 'Being different is the only way I know to fit in with everyone else.'

CUPERTINO
CALIFORNIA

Whinge You, Whinge Me

Nasrudin built a time machine and went back to 1982, so he could buy shares in Apple for next to nothing.

Thrilled with himself, he returned to the present day only to find he was homeless, living on scraps pilfered from rubbish bins.

Enraged, he went to Apple and, after a lot of trouble, somehow managed to get an appointment with the CEO. He explained how he'd built a time machine, bought Apple shares for next to nothing, then returned to the present – hoping to be a billionaire.

The CEO looked at the wise fool in astonishment.

'Surely if you have the ability to make a time machine,' he said, 'and to travel back in time, you could make money without having to resort to such underhand tactics?'

Nasrudin grimaced.

'I came here to whinge about you!' he cried. 'Not for you to whinge about me!'

MASAI MARA
KENYA

The Laughing Hyena

While sitting on a park bench in Sweetwater, Texas, Nasrudin had swallowed a bluebottle just as he was about to take a bite of his sandwich.

He swallowed a pink-toed tarantula to consume the bluebottle.

Then he swallowed a sewer rat to eat the spider.

And he swallowed a banded mongoose to eat the rat.

Finally, he swallowed a blue-ringed octopus to swallow the mongoose.

The wise fool had hoped that the time and trouble he had taken to swallow the octopus would have put an end to his problems.

But, as he was beginning to find out, his troubles were just beginning.

The blue-ringed octopus wriggled and jiggled inside the wise fool so much that there was only one course of action to take...

Nasrudin made his way to Masai Mara down in the Great Rift Valley.

Once there in the tinder-dry grassland, he lay down on his stomach, and he waited...

Sunrise.

Moonrise.

Sunrise.

Moonrise.

Sunrise.

Then, just as he was giving up hope, a laughing hyena hurried out from a nearby thorn bush and charged straight into Nasrudin's open mouth and down his throat.

Swallowing hard, he punched the air and gasped:

'Hoorah! Now, go get that damned blue-ringed octopus, and be quick about it!'

TEHRAN
IRAN

Learning by Example

While on the trail of a lost Stradivarius, Nasrudin had installed himself in a dismal apartment in the Irani capital.

The lodgings were horrific, but even they were not as bad as the landlord. He was the rudest man the wise fool had ever encountered.

One evening, he appeared and invited himself inside the apartment. The wise fool boiled the kettle and brewed up some tea – using his shoe as a pot.

The landlord watched in horror.

'What on earth are you doing?' he asked.

Nasrudin shrugged.

'Well, I noticed how you always use rage in the place of courtesy,' he answered.

'What's that got to do with anything?'

'Well, I've been learning by your example.'

'How so?'

'The shoe is not suited as a pot, but it seems to work – just as rage serves for you in place of courtesy.'

LONDON
ENGLAND

Authenticity

Nasrudin had set himself up as a forger, faking Dutch Old Masters.

Although he'd only been painting by numbers until a few weeks before, his copies were astonishing. Indeed, they were so perfect, other forgers declared that the copies were better than the originals.

Delighted at seeing one of his forgeries, a Vermeer, having been put up for auction at Christie's in South Kensington, the wise fool went along to the sale.

Even though the guide price was astronomical, a rumour was circulating that it was a fake.

As a result, no one at all bid.

Sitting at the back of the room, Nasrudin felt affronted, as though his work was being considered worthless.

In a fit of unwise rage, he leapt to his feet and yelled:

'I know for a fact it's an original!'

From the podium, the auctioneer peered out over the sea of heads.

'Might I enquire, sir, your connection with this painting?'

'I can vouch for its authenticity as a genuine Vermeer,' Nasrudin answered boisterously, 'because I painted it myself!'

NICE
FRANCE

Finder's Reward

Nasrudin was hurrying all over town, gluing posters to walls and lampposts – posters offering a hundred euros to anyone who found him.

A local man happened to be passing. He saw the wise fool rushing about, papers in one hand and a pot of glue in the other. Having befriended the foreigner a few weeks before, he asked what he was doing.

'I've lost myself, so I'm offering a reward to anyone who finds me.'

'How could you lose yourself?' the local asked in bewilderment.

'I don't know. One minute I was right there with myself and the next minute, I was gone.'

The local man blinked hard.

'The thing about being yourself,' he said, 'is that you can't lose yourself.'

Nasrudin balked at the news.

'Oh, yeah! Well tell me where I am, then!'

'You're right there.'

Nasrudin gasped.

'So I am!' he screeched. 'Thank you so much! Here's your hundred euros!'

MENLO PARK
CALIFORNIA

Knowing Me, Knowing You

Famously indecisive, Nasrudin had struggled to make up his mind his entire life.

And so it was all the more surprising that he agreed so readily to accompany a journalist friend to the Facebook headquarters at Menlo Park, to listen to the firm's founder speak.

Taking his seat in a packed auditorium, the wise fool promised his friend he wouldn't cause a disturbance, as was his way. Along with the accredited members of the press corps, he listened to Mark Zuckerberg in rapt silence.

At the end of the presentation, the press officer invited a handful of questions from the media.

Nasrudin's hand shot up above his head.

A microphone was passed to him.

'Excuse me, Mr. Zuckerberg,' he said politely. 'I've got a question. I can't decide whether I prefer blue or green. Could you tell me which it is?'

Facebook's founder frowned.

'That's not really a matter for us,' he answered awkwardly.

The wise fool shook his head.

'Oh, but I thought it was exactly the kind of thing you'd know.'

'Why d'you say that?'

'Because, as people keep telling me, here at Facebook you know your customers better than they know themselves.'

ACCRA

GHANA

True Love, Found

 asrudin fell in love with a spider that had crawled out of the bunch of bananas he bought in the market.

He called her Esmeralda.

Most of his Ghanaian friends threw up their hands in horror at hearing news of the love affair.

Three of them invited the wise fool for coffee, where the arachnid was the only thing on their minds.

'She'll bite you!' one hollered.

'She'll eat your earlobes while you're asleep!' warned another.

'She'll lay eggs, then you'll be in trouble!' roared the third.

Nasrudin blushed, the spider staring into his eyes from the table-top.

'The thing is that when you find true love, it happens, and there's nothing you can do about it,' he whispered.

The first friend jabbed a hand at the little creature.

'Who's saying that spider's in love with you, anyway?' he asked.

The wise fool sighed.

'No idea,' he answered. 'But, before I work out if Esmeralda has feelings for me, I have to be certain of something else.'

'What?'

'Whether she's a girl spider, or a boy.'

CAPE TOWN
SOUTH AFRICA

The Sitter

 well-known South African artist agreed to paint Nasrudin's portrait, so long as he sat very still and didn't say a word.

Agreeing to the conditions, the wise fool took his place in a plush armchair beside the window in the artist's studio and sat very still.

But, within a minute, he was wriggling and fiddling.

'I just need to get comfortable,' he said.

The artist looked at his subject intently, picked up a brush, and began to paint.

At the end of the session, Nasrudin peeked at the work in progress, and was shocked to see it was a blur – a point he drew to the artist's attention.

'Well, it's your fault for not sitting still!' the painter retorted. 'How can I be expected to do anything more than paint what I see?'

'You could use your imagination,' the wise fool suggested.
The artist huffed.

'A portrait's a true rendition of life,' he answered frostily.

'That may be true,' Nasrudin shot back, 'but even the truest of renditions can be improved with a little imagination from time to time.'

LANGTON GREEN
ENGLAND

Known to All

asrudin based himself in England for many years because he said people there left him alone.

Most of the time he went about in threadbare clothes, with his hair dishevelled and his face unshaven. In other parts of the world he might have been derided for being so shabby in appearance, but in England nobody seemed to care.

While visiting his home in the countryside, a friend once asked whether he wasn't concerned what people thought of his sloppy dress sense.

'They all know me here,' the wise fool replied, 'so there's no point in dressing any better than I do.'

'What about London though?' his friend probed. 'Surely when you're in the capital you should dress better.'

'Whatever for?' Nasrudin shot back. 'After all, no one in London knows me, so there's no reason to dress any better there than I do.'

ELK HORN
ARIZONA

Donkeymanſhip

aving had his donkey shipped west from Central Asia to the United States, Nasrudin set himself up as a cowboy.

On the first day, he rode his animal out to where some other cowboys were taking it in turns to show off their skills.

Each one of the others was a seasoned rancher. Anyone else would have been anxious at having to compete with them.

But the wise fool was as cool as a cucumber.

When it was time for him to demonstrate his skill, he leaned forward and whispered in his donkey's ear.

In a display of horsemanship or, rather, of donkeymanship, his animal did whatever it was commanded to do.

This included dancing a jig, balancing a softball on its nose, whistling a tune, and even climbing a ladder.

Green with envy, the other cowboys demanded to know how the newcomer had managed to train a brawny donkey to perform such amazing feats.

'It was nothing at all,' Nasrudin said modestly.

Having been humiliated, a veteran cowboy from El Paso ordered the wise fool to reveal his methods.

'All right!' Nasrudin said. 'I'll tell you how I could have such absolute control over this creature.'

Leaning forwards, the cowboys listened.

'My secret method is the threat of the sausage factory,' he said.

LONDON

ENGLAND

Trying to Please

asrudin had heard a great deal about the illustrious and ancient Eccentric Club, founded in London in 1781, and so was thrilled to have been nominated for membership.

Having agreed to abide by club rules, he was invited for a formal interview. His friend, who was already a member, suggested that the wise fool dress oddly so as to prove his eccentric credentials.

Accordingly, Nasrudin arrived at the clubhouse in London's St. James's, attired in one of the oddest get-ups ever seen in the hallowed halls of the Eccentric Club.

On his head he wore a stuffed beaver. The creature was, in turn, sporting a bowtie and a tartan kilt. Instead of a suit, the wise fool had dressed in a greased banana costume and was wearing fluorescent penguin flippers on his feet.

The interview sessions were held in pairs.

Nasrudin was invited into the meeting room, where the other candidate was already sitting. Unlike the wise fool, he was dressed in an ordinary tweed suit and looked utterly normal.

Six members of the committee grilled the two candidates with a volley of standard questions.

The first one was to explain in a line or two how eccentric they were.

The man in tweed answered by saying he lived in a home in which all the clocks were always three hours behind the right time, that he slept in a bed adorned with peacock feathers, and that he kept a pet fox.

The details were noted by the club secretary in a leather-bound ledger.

'*Pah!*' Nasrudin blurted, his greased banana costume gleaming in the chandelier-light. 'That's nothing at all! *I* live in a house made from cheese, and I keep a herd of reindeer in my bathroom! As for my bed, it's a bed of nails that's a million feet down a mine shaft under my house!'

The committee warned the applicant that fabrication would have him disqualified.

'I expected more from you people!' he bayed, the stuffed beaver on his head slipping onto the floor.

'What exactly do you mean?' the chair of the committee enquired indignantly.

'It's clear as day that the man sitting beside me is guilty of being boring, while I am guilty of nothing more than trying to please!'

PARIS
FRANCE

Wrong Side of the Mirror

While based in an opulent apartment in the Seventh Arrondissement, Nasrudin woke up one morning and believed that, somehow, he'd become trapped on the wrong side of his bathroom mirror.

All he knew was that he had to get back to the right side of the glass.

So, time and again, he tried to climb over the sink and back through.

But, time after time, he failed and fell to the ground.

After an hour or two of trying, he smashed the bathroom mirror.

By chance, a friend arrived at that moment and found the wise fool in a terrible state – bruised all over and covered in splinters of glass.

'Now I'm never getting back through the mirror,' Nasrudin sobbed, 'I'll be forced to spend the rest of my days out here in limbo. Worst of all, I'll have seven years' bad luck for breaking the mirror!'

'Look on the bright side,' his friend urged.

The wise fool balked.

'What on earth could be the bright side of my terrible predicament? I'm not only on the wrong side of the mirror, but I've got seven years' bad luck, too.'

'It could be worse,' his friend replied cheerily.

'Could it?'

'Of course it could.'

'What could be worse?'

Nasrudin's friend thought for a moment.

'Being hit by a falling meteorite.'

'But that would be different.'

'In what way?'

'Because a meteorite strike is sent by the universe,' the wise fool said. 'Whereas my bad luck happened because I sent it to myself!'

SHIMLA
INDIA

Priorities

Nasrudin was terrified of the dark… so much so that he went to a soothsayer living on a hillside outside the hill-station of Shimla and begged him to banish night altogether.

'With no night, there'll always be daylight, and my phobia will vanish,' he explained.

The fakir looked at the wise fool as though he were mad.

'It will be far easier to cure you of your fear of the dark,' he responded, 'rather than bringing an end to night altogether.'

'That may be the case,' answered Nasrudin, 'but when I do something, I don't believe in doing it in a half-hearted way.'

The soothsayer grimaced.

'Spare a thought for all the people and animals whose lives you'd affect if there was no night.'

'What about them?'

'Well, surely they'll be put out terribly at having night banished, merely because you're fearful of it.'

Nasrudin sighed petulantly.

'All right, well then just make it a little bit dark in the middle of the day. That'll give them all the night they need.'

The fakir rolled his eyes.

'You came here for me to treat your phobia,' he said caustically. 'But it's not the phobia that needs treating.'

'What do you mean?'

'There's another deep-seated disorder that's affecting you.'

'Another disorder? What is it?'

'Chronic selfishness.'

ENGLISH CHANNEL

Thanking Providence

Nasrudin had been smuggled from Central Asia and the subcontinent, then through eleven European countries, and was at last on the threshold of his ultimate destination.

Like everyone else he'd met in the dark world of people-smuggling, the goal was to reach the White Cliffs of Dover where – it was said – a cornucopia of free benefits was awaiting him.

The last stretch of what had been a perilous journey was made in a tiny rubber dinghy, no bigger than a toddler's paddling pool. His spirits buoyed by the sight of the gleaming white cliffs across the straits, the wise fool clambered into the vessel and began paddling like mad.

Unfortunately, the dinghy was riddled with holes, so no amount of optimism would keep it inflated.

Very soon, it was overrun with water.

Nasrudin's high spirits were dashed and, in a moment of rage, he cursed Providence for luring him from the safety of his village.

At that moment, there was a blinding flash of light, and a towering jinn appeared.

Hovering above the waves, its voice was like thunder:

'I have been asked by Providence to come and give you a little help,' he boomed.

Nasrudin couldn't believe his luck.

'Thank you! Thank you, O Great Jinn!' he shrieked.

Bowing his head, the spirit regarded the water-logged dinghy and rolled his eyes.

'Shall I transport you in the blink of an eye to the shore of the White Cliffs yonder?'

The wise fool was about to nod, but he remembered his manners.

'First things first,' he cried. 'Please go and thank Providence for thinking of me in my moment of anguish!'

Another blinding flash of platinum light came and went, leaving the unfortunate migrant alone in the dinghy.

Up to his neck in water, Nasrudin waved his fist at the sky.

'Providence! If you can hear me, I'm taking my gratitude back!'

TUNBRIDGE WELLS
ENGLAND

What Matters

Covid-19 was raging, and all anyone was thinking about was getting their vaccinations.

Despite his uncertain status with the authorities, Nasrudin was offered an injection. Once the dose had been administered, he was presented with an impressive-looking certificate, confirming that he was now protected.

Eager to show off, he hurried over to a friend's house.

'I've just had the vaccination!' he cried. 'Those wretched little enemy cells won't get into me!'

'I had the vaccination, too,' his friend said – expecting the wise fool to be pleased.

'Let's see your certificate.'

The friend duly took out a little card.

'*Hah!*' Nasrudin scowled. 'My certificate's much more elaborate than that! So, I'm much better protected!'

The friend frowned.

'It's not about the certificate... but rather the vaccine they injected into your arm.'

'How can you say such a thing?!'

'Because the certificate has nothing to do with it.'

'Of course it has.'

'How can you be so sure?'

'Because if it didn't matter they wouldn't make certificates at all.'

VICTORIA FALLS
ZIMBABWE

Barrel Behaviour

In a career as a circus performer, Nasrudin travelled to Victoria Falls.

With much fanfare, he climbed into a barrel and jumped over the immense cascade of water.

Hired locally, a support team hurried downstream and began the search for the inimitable performer.

But, to their shock, they couldn't locate the barrel.

Fortunately, one of Nasrudin's oldest friends happened to have watched the death-defying spectacle.

'Go upstream,' he said.

'Whatever for?' the support team chief asked in bewilderment.

'Because the man who jumped over the waterfall isn't a usual performer... it's Nasrudin.'

An hour later, having done as was suggested, the barrel was located a distance upstream.

Nasrudin was pulled out, battered and bruised, but alive.

'How come the barrel was washed upstream?' the team leader asked in bewilderment.

The wise fool gave him a sideways glance.

'Who ever said that one barrel has to behave like another?'

TANGIER

MOROCCO

Demons of Cyberspace

However hard he tried, Nasrudin couldn't work out how to use the internet.

Whenever he sent an email, it vanished into the ether, never to be delivered to the intended recipient.

Meanwhile, every child the wise fool encountered was happily sending emails and surfing the internet without any trouble at all.

Having worked himself into a frenzy of rage, Nasrudin went into the kitchen of the house he'd rented in the old medina, grabbed two saucepan lids, and then climbed up on the flat roof of the terrace.

Then, with all his strength, he banged the lids together like cymbals.

It wasn't long before a neighbour cried out, demanding to be told what he was doing.

'I'm simply chasing away the demons in cyberspace!'

'But there aren't any demons in cyberspace.'

'I know that, and you know that,' Nasrudin replied impatiently. 'But believing in them for a few minutes from time to time helps me get through the challenges of modern life!'

ULAANBAATAR
MONGOLIA

Weapons of Choice

 uring solo travels in Mongolia, the wise fool had experienced more than his fair share of misfortune.

While crossing the steppe on horseback, two of his animals had gone lame.

Then, he'd been poisoned at a well of brackish water.

After that, while camping in the middle of nowhere, he was robbed in the night.

The last straw was when, on the southern bank of the Zavkhan River, he was challenged to a duel by a local landowner.

The man who had thrown down the gauntlet was feared by everyone for miles around.

'He's killed a hundred men!' one villager informed Nasrudin.

'He can stop an enemy's heart merely by staring into his eyes,' said another.

The night before the duel, the wise fool repaired to his yurt and calmed himself by reading an old book of Mongolian culture he'd brought along.

At midnight, a muffled exclamation of rapturous joy was heard to ring out from the yurt.

The next morning, Nasrudin was up bright and early, and appeared to be in the very best of spirits.

'Aren't you fearful that you're about to be slain?' asked one of the villagers.

'Not in the least,' responded the wise fool.

'But he's never lost a duel,' another quipped.

'Well, there's always a first time for everything!' Nasrudin cackled.

An hour after that, the farmer who'd challenged the traveller to the duel strode out of his yurt, glared at his opponent, and then at the assembled crowd of villagers.

'Are you ready?!' he bellowed.

'Absolutely,' Nasrudin replied, a book in his hand.

'You'd better put your book away,' the farmer snarled, 'because you're about to die!'

Turning to page 235, Nasrudin read:

'It says here that, under standard Mongolian culture, the person who has been challenged to a duel is permitted to choose the weapons that'll be used.'

'That's right,' snapped the farmer, 'so choose your weapons!'

NASRUDIN'S PEREGRINATIONS

Nasrudin held up two pairs of running shoes. 'These are my weapons of choice!'

MEXICO CITY
MEXICO

Other Side of the Gate

ne afternoon, while strolling through the leafy Chapultepec Park in the Mexican capital, a conman approached Nasrudin.

'Señor,' he lisped, 'I have here in my hand the ancient title document of the Palacio Nacional, the Presidential Palace… a document that dates back to the time of the Aztecs. If you buy it from me, you will be the rightful owner of the palace.'

His eyes wide with excitement, Nasrudin enquired how much the salesman was asking for the title deed.

'Someone just offered me a thousand dollars,' he answered. 'But I turned him down.'

'Why?'

'Because he did not have noble blood.'

'Well, neither do I,' said Nasrudin.

'Of course you do, señor… look at your long aristocratic nose and your deep-set eyes. They are the mark of royalty!'

'What's the lowest price you'll go to?' the wise fool asked.

'Twenty dollars.'

Fumbling in his pocket, Nasrudin pulled out a used twenty-dollar bill and handed it over.

Unable to believe his luck, he went straight to the Palacio Nacional and called through the bars for the guards to unlock the gates.

Almost instantly, a sentry in an official uniform marched up and ordered the foreigner to stop threatening, or else he would be arrested.

'I'll have you know that I just purchased this building from a gentleman in the Chapultepec!'

'I won't tell you to leave again!' the soldier bellowed.

Nasrudin waved the title deed and his fist.

'Be careful how you address me!' he warned. 'Or I'll have you posted to the desert when I'm on the other side of this gate!'

BUENOS AIRES
ARGENTINA

Personality Swap

Nasrudin had been lured to the Argentine capital by the news that there were more psychologists registered in the city than anywhere else on earth. Known for his many neuroses, the wise fool was thrilled.

The day after arriving, he was lying on the couch of a leading psychologist off Avenida Santa Fe.

'What is the nature of your disorder?' the doctor enquired studiously.

'Well,' Nasrudin explained awkwardly, 'I get fantasies.'

'What kind of fantasies?'

'Fantasies that I'm a psychologist, like you.'

'Really?'

'Yes, doctor.'

'Tell me more.'

'Well, just this morning I fantasized I was an Argentine psychologist who was observing a patient as you are observing me right now, in an office just like this.'

'I've got an idea that I think will help you,' the doctor said. 'I'd like you to sit here in the chair, and I shall lie down on the couch.'

'You mean, we'll do role reversal?'

'Yes, that's right.'

A minute later, Nasrudin was in the chair, pad in hand, and the psychologist was lying outstretched on the couch.

'You have a most interesting disorder,' the doctor said, even though he was now lying on the couch.

'But… but…'

'But what?'

'But it's *not* a disorder!' Nasrudin stammered. 'It's reality!'

Lying back, the doctor cleared his throat.

'You must remember that it is *me* who is the psychologist,' he said sternly, 'and *you* are the patient.'

The wise fool cackled with laughter.

'That's a good joke!'

'Oh, but it's not a joke.'

'Of course it is,' Nasrudin replied. 'After all, I'm sitting in the chair and you're on the couch.'

The psychologist got up. 'Get back on the couch.'

Nasrudin did as he asked, and the psychologist sat back down on the chair.

'Again, *I* am most definitely the doctor and *you* are the patient,' the psychologist said firmly, 'and you must always remember that.'

'Yes of course you are,' Nasrudin answered. 'At least for the purposes of our session. You're in the chair and I'm on the couch. That's how I always arrange it when doing role play with my patients.'

YAKUTSK
RUSSIA

Russian Roulette

A mid a journey of extraordinary hardship, the wise fool arrived at Yakutsk in eastern Siberia.

With no money for food, let alone a bed for the night, he found himself begging on the streets. As he huddled in a doorway, a passer-by approached.

Hoping for a coin, the wise fool put out his hand, his fingers frozen with cold.

'I shall give you all the money you need,' the man said. 'But you'll have to earn it.'

'As you can see, I'm in no position to negotiate, and so I will do anything if it means a warm meal, and somewhere to sleep for the night.'

The benefactor led Nasrudin around the corner.

Soon they were sitting together in a restaurant, the aroma of delicious roasted meat wafting through from the kitchen.

'What is it you want me to do?' the wise fool asked, so that he could get it over with and then feast.

'Play a game with me,' the man replied.

'A game? What game?'

'A game of Russian roulette.'

In any other circumstance, Nasrudin would have turned and fled, but such was his hunger that he agreed. Accordingly, he watched as the man took out a revolver, loaded a single bullet, and spun the barrel.

'D'you want to go first, or second?' he asked.

'First,' Nasrudin replied. 'I always go first.'

'*Always*?'

'Yes, always.'

'How many times have you played Russian roulette before?'

The wise fool thought for a moment.

'Oh, hundreds,' he answered absently. 'Maybe even thousands.'

The other man seemed impressed.

'And, pray tell, what's your secret to surviving… good luck?'

Nasrudin rubbed a thumbnail to his cheek.

'Quite the opposite,' he countered. 'You see, my survival has relied on terribly bad luck.'

'How can such bad luck have kept you alive?'

'The kind of bad luck that always seems to put a bullet in my opponent's head rather than mine!'

HAVANA
CUBA

Perfectly Crab

asrudin was seen walking sideways up and down
the beach.

A fisherman asked what was going on.

'I'm learning to think like them,' the wise fool responded.

'Like who?'

'Like crabs.'

'Why?'

'So I understand them, and catch them like no man has
ever caught them before!'

'But why don't you just go and buy a crab net and some
bait?' the fisherman asked.

Nasrudin laughed at the thought of doing the obvious.

'Unlike other fishermen,' he said conceitedly, '*I* am a
perfectionist.'

PARIS
FRANCE

The Real McCoy

Although conscious of the fact he was not a born artist, Nasrudin relocated to the French capital, and set himself up in a studio on the Left Bank.

Having dressed the part, in a striped shirt and a black beret worn at a slant, he heaved his heavy easel to the Beaux Arts quarter early one morning.

Whereas all the other street artists exhibited the most fabulous work, Nasrudin was conspicuous for the astonishingly poor nature of his oeuvre.

All day long, groups of tourists sauntered by. And, without exception, they lavished praise on the wise fool's competitors. Never once did they stop to admire his work.

By late afternoon, Nasrudin's ready smile was waning.

On hearing an American tourist complimenting another artist's sketches, the wise fool marched over and made his feelings known.

'How come you didn't check out *my* work?!' he demanded.

'Because,' the American answered sharply, 'we're only interested in the real McCoy.'

Nasrudin recoiled.

'If anyone here is the real McCoy, it's me!'

'No offence,' the tourist quipped, 'but when you see the real McCoy, you recognize it.'

'And how's that?' Nasrudin spat.

'Because the real McCoy doesn't have to tell you he's the real McCoy – that's why!'

THE SUNDERBANS
INDIA

The Tiger

A little time passed after Nasrudin swallowed the laughing hyena   time in which his digestive tract gurgled and groaned as it had never gurgled and groaned before.

The wise fool was considering an operation to root out the hyena, the octopus, the mongoose, the rat, the spider, and the bluebottle.

But the thought of being sliced open with a scalpel was too terrible for Nasrudin's delicate nerves.

So he went to the Sunderbans instead.

A vast marshland in India's north-east, the region was said by one and all to be populated by the wildest tigers in existence.

Having paid an especially brave boatman to paddle him out into the marshes, Nasrudin lay on his stomach, opened his mouth, and waited.

He waited, and he waited.

And he waited.

Then, just as he was wondering if there were any predators there at all, a huge male tiger sprang from the reeds and jumped down Nasrudin's throat.

Leaping up, the wise fool thrust a hand in the air and cheered.

'Paddle us back to the shore at once!' he bawled. 'And put your back into it!'

The boatman paddled as hard as he could, but his craft hardly moved.

'I don't understand how we are not moving,' he said.

'It's because you're not strong,' Nasrudin replied. 'And because I have a little added weight. You may not realize it, but you are rowing you and me, and a tiger, a hyena, an octopus, a mongoose, a rat, a spider, and a damned bluebottle… which has so much to answer for!'

BUENOS AIRES
ARGENTINA

Faster Than Fast

Nasrudin had enjoyed a long day exploring the backstreets of Buenos Aires and was just crawling into bed when there was a knock at the door of his hotel room.

Opening it, he found a ragged man with a revolver in one hand and a sack of money in the other.

'Señor, please help me!' he exclaimed. 'I've just robbed a bank and the police are chasing me.'

Having been a fugitive himself at one time on his travels, he let the man in and slammed the door.

'I'll protect you, my friend!' he cried.

Five minutes of silence passed.

Then the police pounded at the door.

'Open up in the name of the law!'

The fugitive was shaking. Despite feeling fear as well, Nasrudin kept his calm.

'I promised to protect you,' he affirmed, 'and that is what I shall do.'

The police thumped at the door, louder than before.

'If you don't open up at once,' one of them called, 'we'll knock the door in!'

'He's not here!' Nasrudin yelled.

'Who isn't?'

'The man you're searching for.'

'How d'you know we're searching for someone?'

'How do you know that I know?' asked Nasrudin.

PARIS
FRANCE

Roller Rink Art

Nasrudin made his way through security at the Louvre as soon as the museum had opened.

While other visitors were gazing at the paintings, the wise fool clipped roller-skate wheels to his shoes. Then, to the utter consternation of the guards, he began zigzagging at top speed through the galleries, whooping at the top of his voice.

More and more members of staff laid chase.

Within a few minutes they had arrested him.

'What on earth were you thinking?' the security chief demanded to know. 'Skating like that in the most sacred museum in the world breaks a thousand rules!'

'Museum?' answered Nasrudin in confusion. 'I assumed it was a roller-skating rink with an art show combined!'

OAKLAND
CALIFORNIA

Big Picture Thinking

asrudin had heard stories of how all the most successful tech firms in Silicon Valley had started in a garage.

So, hoping to follow tradition, he rented a fabulous quadruple garage with a tiny apartment attached.

Once the lease was signed and secured, the wise fool kitted out the garage with workbenches, computers, water fountains, ambient lighting, and even a punch-bag.

A few days passed in which the wise fool added the final details.

Then, when everything was perfect, he called his best friend to come and check the garage out.

'It's amazing!' his pal exclaimed. 'Not even Jobs and Wozniak had a space like this. Tell me, what's your plan for it?'

'What d'you mean?' Nasrudin said.

'Well, now that you have a top-end garage, what's the start-up you're planning?'

Nasrudin had spent so much time getting the garage right that he hadn't given any thought at all into what he'd do there.

'Unlike the trailblazers who came before me,' he said, 'I'm getting the little details sorted, so the big picture takes care of itself.'

BERLIN
GERMANY

The Procrastination King

Nasrudin was supposed to be writing a report on German statistics, but he found the subject so tedious that he started writing a poem about porcupines instead.

But, after working on the poem for an hour or so, he was so bored with it that he went over to the sink and began doing the washing up.

Then, tiring of doing that, he picked up three oranges and began teaching himself how to juggle.

And, finding it far harder than he imagined it would be, he tried to hold his breath and count to a hundred.

Through the afternoon he started on at least fifty things, but found each one was more tedious to master than the thing before.

Finally, he went back to the report on German statistics.

'Don't pretend to me that you're interesting!' he growled at the page of numbers. 'Because I know you're boring as sin. I'm only doing you because everything else I can think of is even more dreary than you!'

NAPLES
ITALY

All in the Details

After hunting Nasrudin for weeks across southern Italy, the Neapolitan Mafia caught him, took him to a building site, and began making him walk the plank over wet concrete.

'How can you end my life?' he shrieked.

'Because you insulted Don Lambrusco! And anyone who insults Don Lambrusco is as good as dead!'

'But...'

'But *what*?!'

'But, if you kill me, you'll never find out the location of the treasure!'

'What treasure?'

'The one that only I know about!'

The hitman gave a signal for the condemned man to pause.

'Where's this treasure, then?' he asked.

'Not far from here… in the mountains.'

'And how are you expecting us to believe you?'

Nasrudin put his hand on his heart.

'I have no need for a vast treasure,' he said. 'Imagine what problems it would give a man like me.'

'So, how are you expecting us to find it?'

'I'll draw you a map.'

Ten minutes later, the wise fool was off the plank with a pencil in hand and was sketching out a map on a sheet of paper.

'There you are,' he said jubilantly. 'Take that to Don Lambrusco, and he's likely to kiss your cheeks.'

The hitman snatched the map away and held it to the light.

'But there are no names on the map.'

'Names are mere details,' Nasrudin answered, 'as you can see, I've left out a lot of details. If you want names, it's quite easy to fill them in yourself.'

COPENHAGEN
DENMARK

Worry You, Worry Me

Nothing could stop Nasrudin from worrying during the time he spent in Denmark.

The condition was sparked off by the high cost of living in the Danish capital. And although it had started in a modest way, the worrying snowballed.

Within a week, the wise fool was worrying at fever pitch.

The more he worried about how he'd stop worrying, the more he worried.

As time passed, he worried about everything – from waking up in the morning to brushing his teeth, and from chewing with his mouth shut, to the sound his feet made as he walked along the street.

Eventually, he was taken to a doctor.

Looking the patient in the eye, he asked:

'Tell me, what are you worrying about right now?'

Nasrudin gasped.

'I'm worrying about you worrying about me!' he said.

MANHATTAN
NEW YORK

Plan of the Plan

aving left his village and travelled by land across Central Asia, the Near East, Europe, and the Atlantic, Nasrudin eventually reached his ultimate destination – New York City.

From the first moment he was admitted into the United States, he told everyone how he planned to make his fame and fortune.

'By this time next year I'll be a billionaire!' he bragged over and over.

Most of the people he accosted had no time for fools and were keen to be on their way.

The only person who was interested was a bum lying outstretched on a bench in Central Park.

'Fame and fortune?' he said approvingly. 'That sounds big.'

'Oh, yes,' the wise fool answered. 'I'm going to be richer than in my wildest dreams!'

The bum sat up.

'So, what's your plan, then?'

'Just like I told you, it's to become a billionaire.'

'No, no… I mean what's your plan to get rich?'

Nasrudin's expression froze.

'Don't rush me,' he said brusquely. 'That's the plan of the plan. As things stand, I'm still working on the plan.'

PANGUITCH

UTAH

Retrained Hands

While driving cross-country along Highway 66, Nasrudin was stopped for zigzagging all over the road.

The officer who'd pulled him over was wild with anger.

'In forty years patrolling this stretch of highway, I've never seen driving as bad as that!'

Gasping apologies, the wise fool explained that in the land where he was from, everyone drove in that way.

'Well, you're not in your godforsaken country now! D'you understand?'

Nasrudin nodded nervously.

'Sincerest apologies, officer,' he muttered. 'But even though I tried to retrain my brain, my hands are finding it a challenge to learn new ways.'

TUSCAN
ARIZONA

Discount Skunk Hound

Nasrudin had always been a cat-lover, and so it was surprising that, while living in Arizona, he became obsessed with dogs.

He spent all his time learning about rare breeds and ways to teach man's best friend new tricks.

During his dog infatuation, the wise fool was approached by a crook who was in need of some quick cash. Having heard of his preoccupation with rare breeds, he convinced Nasrudin that the skunk he had on a leash was in actual fact an obscure breed of lapdog.

'He's certainly got fine markings,' the wise fool crooned, taking in the white stripe running nose to tail.

'I can see you know your dogs,' the conman answered. 'And that's why I knew you'd be interested in this competition gold-medal-winning skunk hound.'

Thrilled at the flattery, the wise fool enquired about the price.

'I was going to ask $500,' the crook replied, 'but, since you have such a discerning eye, I'm willing to part with her for $250.'

'My very own pedigree skunk hound for half price!' exclaimed Nasrudin, handing over the money.

Ten minutes later, the skunk hound and its owner were ordered to leave a local shopping mall.

'What kind of lunatic would have a skunk on a leash?!' an elderly lady screamed in the parking lot.

'I can't imagine,' Nasrudin responded absently. 'In fact, I'm amazed anyone would ever keep anything but a skunk hound as a pet.'

ELLIS ISLAND
NEW YORK

The Saviour

asrudin was standing at the foot of the Statue of Liberty, a megaphone in hand.

'O mighty saviour of the American people!' he shouted. 'Please go to my village and free it from our tyrannical leader!'

A guard, who happened to be passing, assumed he was witnessing an A-grade imbecile in the flesh.

'What kind of fool are you, yelling at a statue?!'

'No bigger fool than you, for shouting at a stranger and assuming he can understand you.'

'Well, you evidently *can* understand me!'

'That may be true,' Nasrudin answered, 'but you didn't know it was true when you called out to me... just as I didn't know this great statue was rooted to the ground until I reached it a moment ago!'

PARIS
FRANCE

I'm a Bad Toilet

aving heard about the joys of Japanese toilets, the wise fool shelled out a fortune on one when he moved to Paris.

After spending another fortune in paying the one plumber in the city who claimed to know how to plumb the contrivance in, Nasrudin got on with his life.

But all was not well with the upgraded arrangement.

Whenever Nasrudin used the appliance, it either soaked him with water, scrubbed him up and then scrubbed him down, or hosed him down with bleach.

Enraged, he disconnected the toilet from the water and electricity supply. Then, on a sheet of cardboard, he made a sign of shame and hung it above the loo.

It read:

I'M A BAD TOILET AND
I SHOULD KNOW BETTER!

Well aware that the wise fool had no facilities at his home, his friends tended not to visit. The exception was a friend of a friend, who passed by chance.

While Nasrudin was on the phone, he slipped into the washroom and found the sign and the shamed toilet from Japan.

Mentioning the subject during their conversation, the guest enquired as to the problem.

'That damned thing almost killed me!' Nasrudin screamed.

'Do you think it's faulty?'

'Possibly. What's more certain is that it's a rascal. And there's only one thing to do with rascals…'

'Humiliate them with signs?'

'Yes!' the wise fool grunted.

'Might I enquire why you simply don't learn how to use it properly?' the visitor asked.

'A time for that may come in the future,' said Nasrudin judiciously. 'But first the rascal must be punished.'

'Why?'

Nasrudin huffed.

'Well, if he isn't,' he said icily, 'how can he be expected to change his ways?!'

RISHIKESH
INDIA

Donkey Elixir

Deep in the Himalayas, the wise fool came to a cave in which he found a *sadhu*.

The mendicant had not met another human for thirty years and, fearing he was about to expire, he wanted to pass something of value on.

'Many years ago,' the holy man explained in little more than a whisper, 'I was given this phial of liquid by a fakir. He in turn had been given it by another fakir, who had been given it by another.'

Taking it, Nasrudin held it up to the light at the mouth of the cave.

'What's in it?'

The hermit seemed moved at the question.

'It is filled with the Elixir of Eternal Life.'

'You mean, whoever drinks it will live forever?'

'That is so,' the mendicant replied.

'Excellent!' Nasrudin answered. 'I've looked everywhere for a medicine to get a few more years out of my donkey!'

MONROVIA
LIBERIA

Crocodile Curse

asrudin had been in Monrovia for a month, while on the trail of the so-called 'Human Crocodile Society'.

He never managed to catch up with the elusive secret society, but during his research, he was introduced to a leading witch doctor. In one meeting, the wise fool droned on about how he didn't believe in magic and superstition.

'I can see your future in these sheep entrails,' the medicine man said.

Nasrudin gasped.

'Tell me! Tell me!'

'I didn't think you believed in my magic.'

'I don't! But it doesn't mean I can't help but be sucked in.'

The medicine man pulled the entrails apart, his fingers glistening with blood.

'Don't go to the banks of the river at night,' he said.

'Why not?'

'Because you'll be devoured by a crocodile.'

Although mocking the curse of the crocodiles, Nasrudin kept well away from the river between sunset and sunrise.

A little time passed, and the wise fool passed near to where the crocodile lay one afternoon. The sun was glaring down. As it was still many hours until dusk, the wise fool went over.

'You thought you could devour me,' he hollered, 'but I'm far too clever for you, you wretched lizards!'

As he taunted them, the moon slipped across the sun in an eclipse, and Monrovia was thrown into darkness.

Terrified out of his skin, Nasrudin held his hands outstretched to the heavens.

'The crocodile curse!' he bawled. 'How could I have mocked you?! Forgive me! Pathetic wretches like me are all swagger when the sun's warm on their backs!'

TRANSYLVANIA
ROMANIA

Vampire Matters

asrudin was travelling through Transylvania, when he saw an advert for someone to act as Count Dracula at a guesthouse.

Running short on funds, the wise fool enquired, and learned that the hostelry had a distinctive Count Dracula theme.

The beds were coffins, the curtains were sewn shut, and the milk was dyed red. All night, a recording of wailing and the sound of the floorboards creaking was played. The owner of the establishment explained how he was tired of surprising guests by leaping out in the dead of night dressed as Count Dracula.

'I'm not as young as I once was,' he said softly. 'There gets a time when even a would-be vampire must hang up his fangs and his cloak.'

Nasrudin agreed to take the job.

'Before you start,' the owner said, 'it would be best for you to spend a night as a guest, to experience the fear. But, of course, you know I'll be jumping out in the night – so there's nothing to be frightened of.'

That night, the wise fool climbed into the coffin bed and fell into a deep child-like sleep. He dreamt of blood-crazed vampires and of werewolves.

On the stroke of midnight, Count Dracula leapt out from the cupboard, in search of fresh blood.

Even though Nasrudin knew it was the owner of the guesthouse all dressed up, he climbed the walls in fear.

'I know it doesn't make sense!' he wheezed. 'But the part of me that deals with vampire matters is even more gullible than the rest of me!'

HOLLYWOOD
CALIFORNIA

Lopsided Lipo

Nasrudin was terribly overweight – a result of gorging himself on fast food during the months he had spent in the United States.

A friend suggested he visit a cosmetic surgeon in the Hollywood Hills.

'I understand that you differ from other clinics,' he said at the consultation, 'in that you agree to do whatever surgery a client wants.'

Sizing the wise fool up as a potential customer, the surgeon agreed.

'It's not for me to have an opinion on how you should look,' he answered in a silk-like voice. 'After all, it's you who lives in your body, not me.'

'Very well,' Nasrudin said, 'I want the right half of my body subjected to extreme liposuction.'

'And what about the left side?'

'Leave it alone.'

The surgeon nodded and, next day, the extreme surgery was performed.

Once the bandages had been removed, the wise fool looked in the full-length mirror of his hospital room. Anyone else might have screamed, but Nasrudin was thrilled beyond words.

The right side was fatless and svelte, but the left side was still grossly obese.

Bearing in mind that he'd promised not to voice his opinions, the surgeon wished the customer well and watched as he was discharged.

From the moment Nasrudin left the hospital, people stared.

It wasn't long before the wise fool was invited on a chat show, so that the public at large could try and make sense of his lopsided lipo.

The interviewer asked he if had any regrets.

'Not in the least,' he said sternly. 'In actual fact, I'm sure other people will copy me, and do it lopsided as well.'

'So, what's next?'

'Well,' the wise fool replied, 'I was thinking of getting blinded in one eye, and then have one of my ears surgically removed.'

The talk show host flinched.

'What on earth for?'

'As a way of upgrading a system,' Nasrudin said.

'I don't understand,' the chat show host retorted.

'Well, nothing is so important as pushing the boundaries of acceptance within society,' he said.

MALDONADO
ECUADOR

The Reticulated Python

 eeply vexed at having been swallowed, the tiger leapt from side to side, shredding Nasrudin's intestines.

In agony, he asked a godman in Kolkata what to do.

'You must go to the jungle!' the guru exclaimed.

'Why?'

'Because the only hope for curing your condition is to track down a great serpent and to swallow it before it swallows you.'

Nasrudin retched.

'I'm tired of swallowing things,' he said feebly. 'I've already swallowed more than my fair share of animals.'

The godman pointed at Nasrudin.

'The jungle is waiting for you!'

So, taking the advice, and paying the holy man with a handful of coins, the wise fool set off to the jungle.

After a long, zigzagging route, he reached Maldonado in the Upper Amazon.

As if cued to do so, a jungle guide lurched out from a bar and offered his services. Drunker than drunk, he was a washed-up American, a veteran of free love, sit-ins, little pink pills, and of Vietnam.

'It may sound curious to your ears,' Nasrudin explained, 'but I need to find a reticulated python and swallow it before it swallows me.'

'You've come to the right man and the right place!' the guide snapped, falling into a heap on the ground.

An hour later, the guide was sober – or at least he was as sober as he'd been in years – and was leading the way through the undergrowth in search of a python.

By nightfall, the guide and the wise fool were standing at the base of a towering sumauma tree.

Rather than lie outstretched on the forest floor, Nasrudin stretched his arms around the trunk of the tree, opened his mouth, and waited.

The cacophony of the jungle night was drowned out by the sound of the Vietnam vet ranting on about the adventures of his life.

Then, an hour before dawn, a massive reticulated python slunk down from the high branches and straight down Nasrudin's throat.

Having gasped for air more deeply than he'd ever gasped for air before, the wise fool pushed himself away from the tree and cried:

'Let's get out of here before the damned snake has second thoughts and wants to come back out!'

AQABA
RED SEA

Shark Think

Nasrudin was a keen scuba diver, and was frequently seen descending into the deep waters of the Red Sea, twin tanks of air strapped to his back.

One day, while diving alone, a shiver of sharks surrounded him. Rather than being menacing, they seemed to welcome him. Overcome with a sense of poignancy for the moment, the wise fool swam off with the sharks.

Although he couldn't speak their language, he found that he could understand exactly what the group was thinking. As he swam in and out among them, he came to understand that they were planning to attack another diver.

Instead of begging them to abandon the plan, or warn the diver, Nasrudin went along with them on the attack.

Minutes later, a diver who had tanks strapped to his back, just like the wise fool, was badly mauled.

Miraculously, the diver survived and during his recuperation, Nasrudin paid the man a visit.

'I feel terrible,' he said. 'You see, I was caught up in the sharks' group think, powerless to break free.'

'But they attacked me and you did nothing to stop them!' the diver exclaimed.

'I know… but, as I told you, I was sucked into their vortex. For all intents and purposes, I was a shark as well.'

The injured diver managed a hint of a smile.

'Well, thank God you've regained your senses,' he said. 'And you're no longer suffering from shark think.'

Nasrudin seemed bashful.

'That's where you're wrong,' he said. 'After the attack, they made me "Shark Protector of the Land". They sent me here today, to finish off the work they began.'

With that, the wise fool lunged at the diver, and bit him hard on the arm.

AUSTIN
TEXAS

Classic Nasrudin

Nasrudin had heard how, as a ruse to increase sales of the original formula, Coca-Cola had launched the new version of its name-brand drink in the 1980s.

The ruse had worked, with sales of the Classic formula selling better than it ever had before.

Drawing all kinds of conclusions from Coke's initiative, the wise fool set about emulating it.

Even though he was very well liked, he always thought he could be yet more popular. So, one day, he started acting in a way that was the exact opposite of his normal behaviour.

When his friends wished him good morning, he leered at them, screaming he hoped they'd rot in hell.

On receiving invitations to dinner, he snapped back that he'd rather die than eat the poisonous food on offer.

And when Christmas came around, the wise fool smashed up all the gifts he was sent and returned them to his friends.

Needless to say, Nasrudin's popularity suffered.

A week or two after Christmas, he announced that everyone could relax, because he was no longer the New Nasrudin but, rather, had returned to being his old self – Nasrudin: The Original.

Unlike the Coca-Cola ruse, the wise fool's plan was not a success.

Years after the Original Nasrudin was back, his friends still crossed the road to avoid him.

UPPER AMAZON
PERU

Quality Over Quantity

aving watched a documentary about the Upper Amazon, Nasrudin started to learn Resìgaro, a language spoken by only a handful of people.

The draw of the language was largely that it was so rare. The wise fool imagined that in being so it would be somehow exclusive, and that the conversations in Resìgaro would be sublime.

For ten years, the wise fool struggled to master the language, learning it from recordings found in a linguistic archive. By the time he arrived at the village where Resìgaro was spoken, only one native speaker survived. An elderly woman with no interest in meeting outsiders, she shunned the wise fool.

Despondent at having invested so much time learning the language, Nasrudin made the long journey out of the jungle.

One night in Cusco, someone asked what lesson he'd taken from his adventure.

'I advise anyone thinking of learning a language,' he said, 'to make sure they really want to talk to the people who speak it.'

LONDON

ENGLAND

The Living Statue

The wise fool was walking through Trafalgar Square when he spotted a man walking towards him who'd been at school with him.

The one person stupider than Nasrudin, he was an utter imbecile and a bore.

Thinking fast, the wise fool climbed up onto the empty 'fourth plinth' and struck a pose.

Reaching the plinth, the man from the same village gaped in amazement.

'That looks like Nasrudin!' he bellowed. 'I wonder how he got so famous that they gave him his own statue here in central London?'

Frozen in a pose, the wise fool couldn't bear it any longer.

'They made a statue of me here in Trafalgar Square,' he bellowed, 'because I'm so incredibly wonderful, and not stupid and boring like you!'

'Well, if I'm so stupid and boring,' the man said, 'how can you explain why I'm a multi-millionaire?'

As Nasrudin did a double take, he noticed that the man from his village was indeed dressed well. He was wearing an exquisite handmade suit and was carrying a hand-tooled briefcase.

Climbing down off the plinth, he pretended he'd only been joking, then asked how his dear friend had come into such wealth.

'I can't quite remember,' the man answered.

'But you must have some idea.'

'That's the strange thing. I don't – in fact I don't remember anything at all.'

'D'you know anything?'

The man nodded.

'Yes. I know that I'm filthy rich.'

'How much money d'you have?'

Checking an app on his phone, he squinted at the miniature screen.

'£145,494,846.03.'

'I'm thrilled for you.' Nasrudin said. 'Well, I have to be going, because I'm selling my plinth here to a billionaire tonight.'

Cocking his head back, the friend looked up at the plinth and panned round, as he admired its commanding position in Trafalgar Square.

'What a wonderful plinth,' he said. 'And, as the owner, are you allowed to stand up there any time you like?'

The wise fool gave a double thumbs up.

'I stand up there on my days off,' he said. 'It explains how you came to find me here today.'

'I know it's none of my business, but since we're such old friends, could I ask how much a plinth like that, in a place like this, goes for?'

'It's not cheap,' Nasrudin replied. 'Not cheap at all.'

'I can't imagine it would be. What are we talking…?'

Nasrudin rolled his eyes.

'I shouldn't tell you,' he said in a whisper, 'but the billionaire's paying me £145,494,846.03.'

The friend checked his phone again.

'That must be a sign from God!' he howled.

'What d'you mean?'

'Well, it's exactly the same amount of money I've got in my account.'

'Gosh, what a coincidence.'

'My old friend, if I were to match the billionaire's offer, would you sell the plinth to me?'

Nasrudin sighed.

'All right. So long as you don't try and sell it to anyone else.'

'Agreed.'

The wise fool provided his bank details.

When the transfer had been made, the friend climbed up onto the plinth.

'At last there's meaning to my life!' he cried out, the words blown across the square on the wind.

Melting into the shadows, Nasrudin watched as the man from his village was arrested.

'It might have been a little pricey,' he said, 'but at least he's having an experience he's sure to remember.'

MANHATTAN
NEW YORK

The Nocturnalist

Nasrudin watched a programme about night-vision goggles used by the military and spent all his money on a pair – sourced from a site on the dark web.

Having used them for an entire week, he realized they allowed him to see even better than usual.

An additional benefit was that, by living a completely nocturnal life, he didn't have to deal with queues on public transport, in shops, or anywhere else.

At first, the wise fool tried to persuade his close friends in New York to follow his trend, but they all laughed at him and refused.

Unfortunately though, the one person he loathed in life – a consummate bore – had overheard his effusive rants to embrace a nocturnal lifestyle. Following the advice, he bought a pair of the goggles and became a 'nocturnalist', too.

One night, while the wise fool was quietly strolling the empty streets of Fifth Avenue, the bore bounded up to him.

'It's me! It's me!' he hollered. 'I should have switched to nocturnalism years ago! And as you're the only person I know who's awake at night, I'm hoping we'll become best friends!'

Nasrudin groaned.

'Listen!' he snapped, with uncharacteristic bluntness. 'I'm enjoying the solitude. So, if you don't go back to daytime living, I'm going to have to do something drastic.'

'Drastic?'

'Yeah.'

'Like what?'

Huffing and puffing, Nasrudin thought for a minute.

'Like getting the sun to swap round with the moon and stars,' he said.

RENO

NEVADA

Blind Man's Buff

ored to death while waiting for the buffet breakfast bar to open at a diner, Nasrudin challenged his donkey to a game of his own version of blind man's buff.

Tearing off the poor animal's tail, he covered his eyes, and tried to stick the dismembered tail back in place with a drawing pin.

Needless to say, the game caused the poor donkey a great deal of grief.

'*Hah!*' the wise fool cackled scornfully after half an hour of playing. 'I won! I won!'

The donkey didn't reply.

'You're such a sore loser!' Nasrudin hissed. 'At least I'd expect you to thank me for making you whole again!'

DESERT SPRINGS
AUSTRALIA

High-tech Hat

While spending time in the Outback, Nasrudin was presented with a hat by his friend, Crocodile Mike, on whose porch he liked to wait out the blistering afternoons.

Corks were dangling on strings around the brim.

The corks kept some flies away from the face below the brim, but not all.

One afternoon, when the heat was especially oppressive, the wise fool had an idea. He scurried off into the undergrowth with a handful of sausage, a shoebox, and a sock.

An hour later he returned, having trapped half a dozen geckos.

Without even pausing to wipe the sweat from his brow, Nasrudin swapped the geckos with the corks, hanging them around the brim from their tails.

With a satisfied sigh, he took his place on his friend's porch.

'Strewth!' Crocodile Mike exclaimed. 'What ya do that for, Nasrudin?!'

The wise fool gave his friend a sideways glance.

'Simply upgrading technology,' he said.

BRISTOL

ENGLAND

Twice a Day Time

Nasrudin had run out of funds with which to continue his travels and had nothing to sell.

Nothing, that is, except for his old wristwatch.

An heirloom, the timepiece had been passed down for generations and had been left to him by his father.

Although it was faithfully worn, no one in the family had ever seemed to mind that it didn't work.

Dejected at having to part with the wristwatch, Nasrudin stumbled into a pawnshop on Corn Street, unstrapped the timepiece, and passed it to the manager.

'It's been in my family for generations,' he said glumly.

'But it doesn't work,' the manager replied.

The wise fool frowned.

'It tells the time twice a day, and that's all I ever need it for.'

'The watch is broken,' the manager said, his voice more stern than before. 'If it doesn't tell the time all day and all night, we can't sell it.'

A look of stupefaction descended over the wise fool's face.

'Can you imagine how much a watch that worked all day and all night would cost?' he asked.

KONYA
TURKEY

Wikipedia Masochism

As a fool of international repute, Nasrudin had a Wikipedia page, which detailed his many awards for foolishness and listed the numerous examples of stupidity ascribed to him.

Any other fool would have been pleased to have such a long and well-written Wikipedia page – but the wise fool was frustrated.

He sought out a hacker on the dark web to edit his Wikipedia page.

In yet another display of full-on foolishness, he instructed the contact to say terrible things about him – that he was a fraud, a liar, a cheat, and that he wasn't very foolish at all.

When the revised page went live, another fool asked Nasrudin why he had wanted to be portrayed as unfoolish.

'I just can't help myself,' the wise fool answered. 'It's an example of my masochistic tendencies getting the better of me again.'

KOBE
JAPAN

Improvement

As Nasrudin travelled southwards through Japan on the bullet train to Kobe, he stood out like a sore thumb.

It wasn't just that he looked unlike the Japanese, but that he behaved quite differently to them. Whereas the locals were considerate of their fellow travellers, the wise fool only thought of himself.

He played music very loudly, peeled oranges and dropped the rind on the floor of the carriage, and took off his shoes and socks – exposing everyone else to his foot odour.

Unable to stand it any longer, one of the other travellers plucked up courage and confronted the foreigner.

'Excuse me, sir,' he intoned politely, 'I believe you are a very inconsiderate man.'

Nasrudin burst out laughing.

'Inconsiderate?!' he boomed. 'Fantastic! I'm *thrilled* to be inconsiderate!'

'It is not good to be inconsiderate,' a young lady passenger said curtly. 'It is not good at all.'

'Well,' the wise fool crowed, 'I'd say it's pretty good!'

'It is not,' the lady corrected.

'Ha!' Nasrudin cackled. 'I just came from China, and over there I was called rude, crude, smelly, obnoxious, and all kinds of things worse than that… So, if in your eyes I'm only inconsiderate, I'm certainly improving!'

PYONGYANG
NORTH KOREA

The Greateſt Secret

During his journey through South Korea, Nasrudin inadvertently crossed the DMZ into its northern neighbour.

Within a few minutes of arrival, he was arrested, charged as a foreign spy, and thrown into the deepest dungeon that could be found. Having been chained to a wall, the wise fool was informed that he would now be tortured.

'There's no need to knock me about,' he answered brightly. 'I'll tell you everything I know.'

The chief of the Secret Police, who was present, regarded the prisoner suspiciously.

'And what is it you claim to know, you American spy?!'

Despite being shackled tightly and hardly able to move, the prisoner struggled to stand straight.

'I know the greatest secret of your enemies,' Nasrudin said, 'and I'm more than happy to share it with you. But I have one condition.'

The chief of police drew close.

'What is your condition?'

'That I reveal the secret directly to His Supreme Excellence the President!'

A string of orders were given, keys turned in locks, a bucket of ice-cold water was thrown over the spy, and he was dragged out of the cell.

Within an hour, the chief of the Secret Police led him into the main hall of Residence No. 55, the palace of President Kim Jong-un – in the tunnels beneath which he'd been about to be tortured.

The supreme leader regarded the prisoner with disdain.

'I shall give you fifteen seconds to reveal the greatest secret of my enemies,' he intoned, 'and then you shall be returned to the hole from which you came.'

'But, Your Supreme Magnificence,' the wise fool mumbled, 'how can I be expected to remember the greatest secret while these manacles cut so tightly into my ankles?'

The presidential hands clapped once, and the manacles were removed.

'Now speak the greatest secret without delay!'

'Without delay!' the chief of the Secret Police echoed.

Nasrudin sighed.

'All the threats and yelling I have endured have made me more tired than you could ever know,' he said. 'To pass on the greatest secret, I really would need to be sitting in a comfortable chair.'

Although vexed, the supreme leader clapped his hands, and a Louis IX fauteuil was borne in for the prisoner.

'This is much better,' Nasrudin said, leaning back into the chair.

'Anything else?!' Kim Jong-un snapped sarcastically.

'Well, since you ask, I would very much like to eat a meal. You see, I haven't eaten for ages, and my stomach is grumbling.'

The presidential hands clapped a third time.

An instant later, a fabulous lunch was ushered in. His eyes widening at the sight of such delicious food, Nasrudin feasted, while the president fumed.

'As I have told you,' the supreme leader snarled, 'I shall have you taken back to the dungeon unless you reveal the secret without delay!'

As he bit into a succulent slice of melon, the prisoner managed half a smile.

'But you're doing so well,' he said, the words muffled. 'They're part of a process... a process that was enabling me to trust you.'

Kim Jong-un glowered at the spy.

'Whether you trust me or not is of no interest whatsoever!'

'On the contrary,' Nasrudin riposted, 'I would say that when great secrets are involved, trust is everything. Besides, if I'm given what I need, the secret revealed will sound all the more pleasing to your ears.'

'All right,' the president growled. 'What else do you want before you will reveal what you know?'

The prisoner dictated a list:

'A shave and a hot bubble bath, a massage, and a good night's sleep.'

Nasrudin was marched to a guest room, given a shave, a bath, a massage, and allowed to sleep in a bed fit for a president.

Next morning he was dragged back in front of the supreme leader.

'Are you ready to divulge the greatest secret of our enemies?!'

'More than ready,' the wise fool rejoined.

'Then, speak now! What is it?!'

Realizing he was in a corner and that his time was running out, Nasrudin replied:

'The greatest secret of your enemies is that the earth is flat.'

Kim Jong-un balked at the information.

'But that's not true!' he boomed.

The wise fool shrugged.

'Who said anything about the greatest secret having to be true?'

ABU SIMBEL
EGYPT

Part-time Reincarnation

On a cruise down the Nile, Nasrudin got carried away and told an elderly American tourist that he was the reincarnation of Pharaoh Tutankhamun.

Rather than mocking him as everyone else tended to do, the woman was most impressed. She spent the next day telling everyone on board that Nasrudin was an aristocrat and, as such, ought to be treated with respect.

By the time the boat reached Aswan, all the passengers had turned against the wise fool – all except for the elderly American. She continued to believe his fantastical tales of high pedigree.

A great deal of shouting at Nasrudin followed – so much so that he wished he hadn't spoken so freely.

Hoping to restore calm, the captain came down from the helm.

The details were explained to him.

'If you profess to be the reincarnation of Pharaoh Tutankhamun,' he said, 'you'll have to prove it, or else renounce the claim.'

Nasrudin, who realized he was about to be caught out, swallowed hard.

'This is an unusual matter,' he said. 'You see, although I am indeed the reincarnation of Tutankhamun, at the same time I am not.'

'Make up your mind!' hollered one of the passengers from the back.

'Are you or aren't you?' another bellowed.

'As I have said,' Nasrudin confirmed, 'I am and then again I am not.'

The captain raised a hand.

'Please explain how you could be both at once.'

'Simple,' the wise fool rejoined. 'You see, when talking to the lovely lady passenger who has been so kind to me, I am... and when I am talking to anyone else, I am not.'

'You mean you're a part-time reincarnation of Tutankhamun?' the captain replied.

'Yes, that's right. That's exactly how it is.'

'That's absurd!'

Nasrudin shrugged.

'Absurdity runs deep in my veins,' he said. 'Well, at least it does when I'm being the reincarnation of Tutankhamun.'

SANTA BARBARA
CALIFORNIA

Outwitting Blindness

Even though Nasrudin had 20/20 vision, he assembled a huge collection of books in Braille.

A friend, visiting him at his California home, asked why he was learning to read Braille.

'I'm not learning to read it,' he said.

'Then what's the point of having so many books in Braille?'

'Because, with my luck,' Nasrudin replied, 'if I don't have Braille books, my worst nightmare will come true, and I'll go blind.'

LARABANGA
GHANA

Substitution

While on his travels through West Africa, Nasrudin had heard of a 'Mystic Stone'.

Whenever the sacred object was moved, it would be found to have returned to its original spot, at Larabanga, on the southern edge of the Mole National Park.

Intrigued by mystical matters, the wise fool travelled to the region, pitched his tent, and spent many days studying the stone.

The Mystic Stone awakened in him a deep-seated sense that the forces of nature were calling him in some way.

Although not quite sure how to call back to them, he had an idea.

In the local town of Damongo, he bought a box of golf balls. Then, with each day that passed, he would tie a string around one of the golf balls and hang it from a tree outside his tent.

Day after day, he would hang a golf ball in honour of the Mystic Stone, and the forces which governed it.

Curious as to what the foreigner was doing, the local people would shuffle out of their houses and watch him. Within a couple of weeks, the tree – with its many hanging golf balls – began to attract an audience.

One morning, when Nasrudin was hanging up yet another golf ball, a little girl called out to him:

'What are you doing that for?'

The crowd looked at the foreigner, waiting for his answer.

'Enacting an ancient tradition,' he explained.

'But golf balls are not ancient,' the girl giggled.

'Naturally we don't use golf balls where I come from,' Nasrudin replied. 'But in certain circumstances substitutions must be made.'

CHENNAI
INDIA

Affordability

Few things were more impressive to Nasrudin than the vibrant colours on display in the markets of Chennai.

With an hour to spare before leaving for home, he hurried to the Godown street market, hoping for a bargain with which to please his wife.

By reputation, the wise fool was the epitome of generosity. He would lavish his friends with everything he had. But when it came to his wife, he was far more frugal.

At the first shop he came to, he found a spellbinding array of silk saris. Pulling out the most beautiful one, he asked the price.

'That one is twenty thousand rupees, sir.'

Nasrudin balked at the price.

'I'm not going to pay anything like that!' he exclaimed. 'It's only for my wife.'

The shopkeeper clapped his hands, and an assistant opened a box of less expensive saris.

'These may be more fitting to your budget, sir,' he said.

Nasrudin inspected them, his eyes lighting up as he imagined his wife thanking him upon his return.

'How much do they cost?'

The shopkeeper rubbed his nose.

'Ten thousand rupees each, sir.'

'Ten thousand rupees!' the wise fool gasped. 'That's far more than I have to spend.'

The shopkeeper rolled his eyes.

'Perhaps you will find a bargain to fit your budget a little deeper in the bazaar, sir.'

Giving thanks, Nasrudin pushed on into the market.

Soon, he came to another sari shop. Inside, he pointed to an exquisite length of fabric.

The shopkeeper rubbed his hands together, hoping for sale.

'That one is five thousand rupees, sir,' he said.

'Five thousand rupees! That's a fortune... at least it is where I'm from!' Nasrudin reposted.

'Perhaps you would be more suited to press on deeper into the market,' the shopkeeper said. 'There are saris if you keep going down the lane.'

The wise fool pressed on...

and on...

Eventually, the prices were far lower than at the original shop. Some of the saris were as cheap as five hundred rupees.

But the thought of spending even that much on his wife pained him. Hoping for a last-minute bargain, he went into a sari shop set apart from all the others.

Lost in chill shadow, it was terribly run down.

But, even there, the prices seemed terribly expensive.

Vexed at having wasted so much time and finding nothing, Nasrudin asked the shopkeeper where impoverished people did their shopping.

'Go down that alleyway and turn right at the end.'

'Is it an even cheaper bazaar?' Nasrudin asked expectantly.

'No, sir,' the shopkeeper responded. 'It's a shelter for the homeless.'

TOKYO

JAPAN

Chooje Your Weaponj

Through a series of oversights and unlikely coincidences, Nasrudin's name was added to a list of sumo wrestlers.

Before he could protest, the wise fool found himself in the ring opposite the bulkiest man he'd ever seen.

Shaking like a convict about to be executed, he imagined himself being ground into dust.

The referee asked if he was ready to fight.

'No! No!' he wailed. 'I need a moment.'

'But the audience is waiting, and punctuality is important in the sport of sumo,' declared the referee.

Thinking fast, Nasrudin asked for a measuring tape.

'This is a sumo competition, not a tailor's shop!' the official yelled.

'Please! I can't go on until I've taken a couple of measurements.'

Although vexed, the referee clapped his hands, and a tape was brought. Once in his hands, the wise fool strode over to his opponent and took a variety of measurements, recording them in a notebook.

First, he measured the circumference of his arms. Then he measured his thighs. And, after that, he measured the size of the sumo champion's hands.

All the while, the audience gaped in disbelief at the unusual foreign wrestler.

'Are you ready to begin?!' the referee snapped.

'Not yet… you see, I have to measure myself.'

And with that, the wise fool measured his own arms, legs, and hands.

Having noted the measurements down, he made elaborate calculations.

'Oh dear, oh dear, that's such a great shame,' Nasrudin declared despondently.

The referee demanded to know what the problem was.

'Well,' the wise fool answered, 'unless I am mistaken, any martial art relies on standardization. By this I mean, I wouldn't use a fencing sword in a bout of taekwondo, or a kendo cane in a karate competition.'

'Of course not,' the referee responded. 'Now, can we get on with the wrestling match?'

Nasrudin shook his head from side to side, then held up the figures he'd scribbled down.

'Alas, I cannot fight this man,' he said apologetically.

'Why not?!'

'Because, as you can see from my calculations, we're clearly not armed with the same weapons!'

BAGAN

MYANMAR

Yin and Yang

aving inherited from his uncle a dozen antique Burmese lacquer boxes, Nasrudin continued to build the collection.

Over a period of twenty years, he travelled all over Myanmar searching for fine examples to buy. With time, he was hailed as having the very best collection in private hands.

From time to time, he would open the mansion in which he lived to the public, so that others could admire the fabulous works of art.

On one such occasion, an elderly lady asked why the very finest lacquer box of all was surrounded by exceedingly inferior examples, most of which were broken or clearly second-rate.

The wide fool smiled effusively.

'How can one be expected to appreciate beauty,' Nasrudin answered, 'without knowing what ugliness is?'

YIXIAN
CHINA

Dino Dreams

An amateur dinosaur enthusiast, Nasrudin had heard a rare find had been made in northeast China.

Wasting no time, he hurried to the location to tour the discovery for himself. Getting access to the site with invented credentials, the wise fool was invited to stay at the dig and was given a room of his own.

On the first night he had the most terrible dream – that he was being hunted, and then torn limb from limb, by dinosaurs.

Next day, while the professionals continued with their excavation, Nasrudin hired a blacksmith to put bars over his window.

One of the archaeologists asked what the security was for, after all, there wasn't any danger of break-ins.

'They'll never get in!' Nasrudin quipped.

153

'Who won't?'

'The dinosaurs.'

'Which dinosaurs?'

'The ones that are coming to attack in the night!'

The archaeologist assumed the visitor had been out in the sun too long.

'I can promise you that the only dinosaurs anywhere near here have been dead for millions of years.'

Nasrudin clicked his tongue dismissively.

'That's what *you* may think,' he said. 'So it'll be me who has the last laugh when they devour you as you sleep!'

BEIRUT
LEBANON

Twin Think

O n the third day of ambling around Beirut, Nasrudin had taken a tour of the celebrated Sursock Museum.

A treasure house unlike any other, the collection was located in a magnificent villa. The wise fool was leaving, strolling down the grand imperial staircase. His thoughts on the wonders he had glimpsed inside, he was overcome by the strangest sensation.

Looking sharply to his right, Nasrudin saw a man standing on the very same stair as him. An absolute clone of himself, the figure was dressed identically, too. He was even holding a copy of the same guidebook, open to the same page.

Until that moment, neither Nasrudin nor the other man had known they had an identical twin brother.

Overcome with joy, they hugged tighter than tight.

That evening, Nasrudin and his identical twin dined together. Each one ordered the very same dishes. Then, in exchanging details of their lives, they realized they had both married women from the same town, had children of the same ages, and even hid the same secrets from everyone else.

'This is incredible!' exclaimed the wise fool's twin. 'There's not a single difference between us!'

All of a sudden, Nasrudin's face darkened. Snarling, he waved a fist at his newly discovered brother.

'How could you?!' he bellowed.

'How could I... *what*?'

Nasrudin slammed a fist on the table.

'We're definitely *not* twins!'

'Yes we are!'

'Absolutely not! No! No! No!'

'How can you say such a thing?' the twin asked in horror. 'We look and think identically, and even dress the same.'

'That counts for nothing!'

'I don't understand what's come over you,' the twin gasped.

Straightening his back, Nasrudin pointed a finger at his would-be twin brother.

'I've been trawling through your head telepathically,' he growled, 'and I've found a shocking memory deep in there.'

'Which memory?'

'The one about strawberries and cream.'

The twin rolled his eyes.

'The fact you can read my mind is surely proof that we're identical twins!'

NASRUDIN'S PEREGRINATIONS

Nasrudin shook his head angrily from side to side.

'You might have thought so,' he answered gruffly, 'but, as everyone knows, I *hate* strawberries and cream!'

GOLCONDA
INDIA

Mining Fun

Nasrudin had heard a fortune could be made working at the deep diamond mines at Golconda, and it was only a matter of time before he arrived there looking for work.

The foreman warned him he wouldn't be able to hack it, as he was far too skinny to have a hope of surviving far below the surface. But the wise fool pleaded to be allowed to try his luck.

The official gave a nod.

Nasrudin was lowered down into the mines.

Within an hour, he realized he'd made a terrible mistake, and that the foreman was right – there was no way he was ever going to be able to put up with the hard work or wretched conditions.

'I told you that you wouldn't last a day down there, and I was right!' the foreman jeered.

'Oh, I can stand it,' Nasrudin lied. 'There's no question of that. In fact, I found it very appealing. I loved it… enjoyed every minute.'

'Then why are you leaving?'

'Because it's such wonderfully exhilarating work,' Nasrudin answered, 'that I feel guilty at depriving others of all the fun!'

KHARKHIRAA
MONGOLIA

The Snow Leopard

As anyone who's swallowed a full-grown reticulated python can attest, the reptile caused havoc with Nasrudin's digestion.

With his intestines plugged up, the wise fool sought an urgent remedy.

By chance, he bumped into a hiker he'd once met while trekking in the Andes.

'You need to find a snow leopard,' the hiker asserted.

'Do I?' answered Nasrudin.

'Of course you do!'

So, without dallying another minute, Nasrudin beat a path to Mount Kharkhiraa.

In the depths of winter, the Mongolian peak was shrouded in deep snow. After trekking for weeks on the trail of leopards, Nasrudin reached a cliff. His guide pointed to the top.

'Up there.'

'Up there... *what?*'

'Up there is where the snow leopards live.'

So, donning crampons and grabbing his ice-picks from the gear, the wise fool began to climb.

The guide had been right.

For at the top of the cliff was a cave, from which was coming the sound of young snow leopards at play.

Lying down on the snow, the wise fool opened his mouth and waited for something to happen.

Night fell, and Nasrudin was frozen rock solid. But the warming rays of dawn thawed him and loosened his tongue, which had become stuck to the snow.

Another night of cold and a morning of warmth came and went.

Then, just as Nasrudin could stand no more, a snow leopard cub slunk from the mouth of the cave... and scurried down the wise fool's open mouth.

Jubilantly, the adventurer leapt up, punched the freezing air, and cried:

'Go get that bloody snake!'

GRANADA
SPAIN

Gullible Art

While travelling through Andalucía, Nasrudin was informed the best way to explore the Sierra Nevada was to rent a car.

But, as it was the holiday season, there wasn't a single vehicle to hire in the entire city. He was about to slope back to his hotel when he spotted a terribly run-down car dealership, the forecourt lined with battered cars – each one less costly than the last.

An hour later, Nasrudin was the proud owner of a thirty-year-old jalopy. Not caring what anyone else thought of him, he got into the driver's seat, threw it into gear, and drove away.

Or, rather, he hoped to drive away.

Instead of starting, the car's engine exploded, and the chassis collapsed.

'What's happened?' he gasped.

The salesman who, only minutes before, had been praising the vehicle, seemed alarmingly disinterested.

'God knows,' came his reply.

'Well, what are you going to do about it?' Nasrudin glowered.

'Nothing. You're the owner, so it's *your* problem.'

Closing up the doors to the dealership, the salesman left the customer with the smouldering vehicle, and sloped away to lunch.

Incensed, Nasrudin was going to wave his fists and shout, when he had an idea.

Crossing the road to a framer's shop, he bought an extremely large gold frame, dragged it back across the road, and placed it around the wrecked vehicle.

Within ten minutes a crowd had gathered.

'It's not for sale!' Nasrudin cried out over and over.

'What d'you mean, not for sale?' asked an old lady standing at the front.

The wise fool shook his head.

'Señora, I cannot permit it to be sold, as it's a work of art, the likes of which has never before been exhibited.'

'But that's a clapped-out banger with a frame around it!' a thick-set man at the back called out.

Nasrudin broke into laughter.

'I regret to inform you, señor, that it's the most recent masterpiece by the great Nasrudini!'

A murmur rippled through the crowd.

'Who's Nasrudini?' everyone seemed to ask.

'He's the very greatest modernist of all from the Automotive School.'

'Well, I've never heard of the Automotive School!' shouted an executive.

'How much is it?' a frail-looking man asked.

'Fifteen thousand euros.'

'But that's a fortune to pay for a smashed-up car!'

The wise fool balked.

'I suggest you understand something of key importance,' he said. 'In the eyes of the unenlightened, this may resemble a broken-up vehicle on some levels, but in reality it's an early Nasrudini. And, for that reason, its value is almost incalculable.'

The executive pulled out his chequebook.

'I'll give you the money right away!'

'I'll pay double the asking price!' exclaimed the frail man.

'Name your price, and I'll pay it!' a well-dressed woman at the far side of the crowd hollered.

Just as bidding reached fever-pitch, the used-car dealer returned from lunch.

He seemed amazed to see what was going on.

'I can't believe I've bought an early Nasrudini!' the woman shrieked. 'It'll have pride of place in my art collection!'

As the new owner of the art installation celebrated, the other bidders commiserated, and eventually drifted way.

Never one to miss a trick, the dealer smashed up all the cars on the lot, adorning each one in a gaudy gilt frame.

Despite advertising the vehicles as rare installations in their own right, no one showed any interested at all.

A few days later, it just so happened that Nasrudin was passing the dealership.

Seeing him, the salesman rushed up.

'All I did was to copy you!' he cracked. 'I smashed up the cars and publicized them as art... but no one's even given them a second look.'

Nasrudin slipped the dealer a sideways smile.

'The mistake you made was to imagine people are as gullible as they look,' he said.

SAMARKAND
UZBEKISTAN

Perfectly Suited

While searching for antiques in the Siyob Bazaar, Nasrudin spotted an enormous ivory-coloured object amid an array of worthless clutter.

The size and shape of a beachball, it was warm to the touch.

'What is it?'

'An egg.'

'But what bird could lay such a huge egg?'

The shopkeeper shrugged.

'Haven't any idea… that's why the price is so low.'

'How much?'

The shopkeeper shrugged.

'I'll swap it for your baseball cap.'

Tugging the cap off his head, Nasrudin handed it over, and then borrowed a cart to transport the giant egg back to the house where he was staying.

That night, the wise fool had fitful dreams. He dreamt that a massive bird hatched from the egg and gobbled him up. Then, he dreamt that the lodgings were surrounded by a king who ordered him to be imprisoned for stealing a royal egg.

When he woke up, Nasrudin rushed over to the egg. Although warmer than the evening before, it was very much the same.

Uncertain what to do, he asked his friends.

The first said he ought to cook it and make a huge omelette.

The second suggested he have the contents blown out, and to keep the shell as a lamp.

The third gave him a serious look and said:

'You must hatch it.'

'Hatch it?'

'Yes.'

'But why?'

'Because only then will you know what it is, and what to do.'

So, throwing caution to the wind, the wise fool climbed on the egg and waited.

Days passed.

Then weeks.

He only left the egg when he needed to eat, and for the call of nature.

With time, he managed to sleep as well as in any bed when up on the egg.

His friends grew used to their eccentric friend sitting on the egg when they dropped by.

For many weeks the egg lay dormant, as though nothing was growing inside.

Despite the lack of overt progress, Nasrudin kept sitting. Sometimes he would sing folk songs to the egg, which his grandmother had sung him in his youth. And at other times, he told the egg secrets he'd never revealed to anyone else.

Eventually, one bright morning, there was a dull rumbling, cracking sound.

The egg began to shake, and the wise fool tumbled to the floor.

A moment after that, a primitive, ancient-looking bird appeared.

It had dark feathers, a little red beak, and talons as sharp as razors.

Staring at the creature, his lower jaw hanging, Nasrudin realized that he'd hatched a pterodactyl.

As he stood there wondering what to do, the prehistoric bird nestled up to him, as though he was its mother.

In the days that followed, the pterodactyl paced after him everywhere, and expected him to feed it increasing amounts of meat.

Each day, the creature appeared to grow dramatically in size, until it was as large as an ostrich. Soon, it was consuming so much raw meat the wise fool could stand it no more.

'Shoo!' he yelled at it. 'Go away… it's time you fly off and had a life of your own!'

But the pterodactyl had no intention of going anywhere.

Irked at being impoverished by the foolhardy purchase, Nasrudin strode back to the market stall.

The pterodactyl followed close behind.

'This damned bird has cost me a fortune in meat!' he declared angrily. 'And before that, I spent weeks hatching it! Now, I'm obliged to spend hours each day looking after it, while it enjoys a luxurious prehistoric life!'

'So, what am I supposed to do about it?'

'I want my money back!' Nasrudin snapped.

'You didn't pay any money,' the shopkeeper replied.

'Well, give me back my baseball cap, then!'

'I no longer have it.'

Nasrudin stamped his foot in anger.

'So what are we to do?!'

'Why don't you take it down to the exotic meat bazaar?' the shopkeeper suggested. 'I'm sure there'll be a butcher there ready to give you something for pterodactyl meat.'

The wise fool glowered.

'How dare you talk like that!' he cried. 'He's a pet! Killing him would be murder!'

'You've got fond of him, haven't you?' the shopkeeper whispered, a glint in his eye.

'Of course I haven't,' he shot back. 'But we've spent a lot of time together… both before and after hatching.'

The shopkeeper sighed.

'You should have wondered what was inside the egg before you bought it,' he blustered.

Nasrudin regarded him with rage.

'It's not in my nature to think ahead!' he quipped. 'I think in the present and only the present… which, curiously, is the one quality required to be a mother to a pterodactyl!'

RUB' AL KHALI
SAUDI ARABIA

Just This Once

Regarded as one of the most experienced desert travellers alive, Nasrudin knew more about desert survival than anyone else.

He'd lectured on the psychology of desert travel more times than he could remember, and had been feted for enduring what most others regarded as unendurable.

On the fifth lone crossing of the legendary Rub' al Khali, the so-called 'Empty Quarter' of the Arabian Desert, he travelled not with camels, but with his ever-faithful donkey.

Halfway between the start and the finish, the pair of them were half-dead, the supply of water having run out three days before.

The seasoned traveller had pinned everything on being able to locate the small, brackish oasis that he knew to be near.

As the noon sun arced high above him, Nasrudin spied a sight more glorious than any other he had ever laid eyes upon...

An oasis with towering palms, crystal water, and soft, green grass.

Even though he knew it was a mirage, the wise fool picked up his pace, and staggered purposefully towards the illusion.

His throat too parched to speak, he whispered:

'You damnation from hell, I'll believe in you just this once!'

DUBAI
UNITED ARAB EMIRATES

When High is Low

Nasrudin had heard wonderful things about Dubai, and the fact that it had been transformed from a humble fishing village into an extravaganza of pleasure and delight.

Eager to see it for himself, he arrived by plane, and marvelled at the skyline as a taxi took him into the city.

The driver asked which hotel he was staying at.

'Take me to that one,' he stammered impatiently, pointing to an incredibly tall glass tower.

'That is the Gevora Hotel, sir... the tallest hotel in the world.' A few minutes after that, he was checking in.

Shortly after, he was being escorted to a suite on the seventieth floor.

Leading the way inside, the manager strode over to the window and showed off the view. To his surprise, the guest wouldn't look at it.

Instead, he kept his back firmly turned on the skyline.

'Is there something wrong, sir?' the manager asked.

'Um, er, well... you see... I'm frightened of heights.'

'Then perhaps you would be more comfortable on a floor nearer ground level, sir.'

Nasrudin was about to accept, but then he remembered how word of his phobia had got out before, and how he'd become a laughing-stock.

'No, no,' he said resolutely, 'I am very happy up here in the clouds.'

'Are you sure, sir?'

The wise fool nodded.

'I have a way of dealing with it. You see, I pretend that I'm not high up, but rather very low down... deep under the ground in a mine-shaft. I keep the curtains closed all day, and only go out at night. And, when I take the lift down, I pretend I'm actually going up towards the surface.'

The manager smiled out of pity.

'An excellent plan, sir,' he intoned. 'But if you don't mind me saying, it seems curious.'

'In what way?'

'Well, surely as you know the plan, you won't believe it.'

Straightening his back, Nasrudin grinned with confidence.

'Of course I don't believe it,' he whispered. 'But my phobia does.'

AMSTERDAM
THE NETHERLANDS

Phone Soup

When his son was a teenager, Nasrudin decided to take the boy with him on a journey through Europe.

But, to his disappointment, the child was glued to his mobile phone.

They were staying in a rented apartment in the middle of Amsterdam. Even though there was a wealth of culture to be explored, the boy wanted to stay on the sofa, playing video games on his phone.

Unable to stand it any more, Nasrudin grabbed his son's phone, dropped it in the blender, added a cup of water, and ground it into a thousand pieces. Then, pouring the mess into a bowl, he served it up.

'Here's your lunch! I call it phone soup!'

Although enraged, the teenager didn't react. Instead, he said he wanted to cook a pie.

Thrilled that his son was doing something creative, Nasrudin encouraged the boy to help himself to anything in the kitchen.

That evening, the teenager served his father a rectangular pie with a thick, glazed crust.

'I call it telephone pie,' he said darkly.

The boy's father dug a fork into the dish and struck what he assumed, correctly, to be his iPhone.

'Excellent!' Nasrudin bellowed jubilantly.

'How could you be happy? I baked your phone into a pie!'

'Because, my beloved son, you have understood a fundamental concept.'

'What's that?'

'It is that, while a phone is a phone,' Nasrudin answered, 'it can also be soup, a pie, or almost anything else.'

YELLOWSTONE PARK
WYOMING

Plugging the Leak

As a child, the wise fool had earned himself the nickname 'Do-good Nasrudin', because he'd spend all his spare time helping people sort out the problems in their lives.

Having arrived in the United States, he pledged to continue doing good whenever possible. The way he saw it, every citizen had a duty to leave the world in a better shape than they found it.

One evening, while watching TV in his motel room, Nasrudin watched a nature programme which showed the raw beauty of Yellowstone Park. The camera panned over the magnificent landscape and down onto the immense geyser, Old Faithful.

Having never seen a geyser before, Nasrudin assumed it was an immense leak that was wasting water on a titanic scale.

The do-good spirit roused in him, the wise fool packed his bag and took a series of Greyhound buses until he reached the gates of Yellowstone.

Mindful that the best charity was done anonymously, he waited until night had fallen, then made his way to the geyser. As luck would have it, Old Faithful was paused between eruptions. And, by levering a nearby rock into place, he managed to plug the vent hole with comparative ease.

Next morning, Nasrudin watched from the bushes as his do-good act was discovered. Although not in need of praise, he hoped to catch the sound of appreciation on the wind.

Finding the geyser plugged, a pair of park rangers dragged the rock away. Within an hour, Old Faithful was erupting once again.

Still watching from his vantage point in the bushes, the wise fool rubbed a hand down his chin.

'What a curious nation this is,' he muttered to himself. 'Where water's so plentiful no one cares about plugging such a leak.'

PYONGYANG
NORTH KOREA

Mr. Pea-Brain

Nasrudin saw a news report that the world's first gene-editing clinic had opened in Pyongyang.

Thrilled at the thought of having his meagre stature upgraded, Nasrudin managed to get a visa to the restricted state and was seen at the clinic.

'I understand you can improve me,' he said to the official at the appointment.

'That is right, sir. We can turn you into any version of yourself. We suggest that you simply look through the list of attributes you would like and tick them. We will do the rest.'

More excited than he had ever been, the wise fool ticked the boxes linked to huge muscles, in the hope of being turned into Mr. Universe.

He handed the completed paperwork back to the officials and watched as they conferred with one another.

The chief strode over.

'I must ask you, sir, why you have concentrated entirely on physical attributes, and not on intellectual ones. In most cases, our patients want a mixture of the two.'

The wise fool grinned.

'I'm happy with being a complete idiot,' he said.

'Are you sure?'

'Yes.'

'May I enquire why?'

'Because if I were suddenly a genius,' Nasrudin answered, 'I'd realize what a fool I had been to come here and get turned into Mr. Universe.'

TBILISI
GEORGIA

Staying on Track

aving won the Stupidest Man in the Region contest, Nasrudin was beside himself with delight.

He managed to beat his closest rival by failing to remember his name, by confusing onions with light bulbs, and for asking a garden chair to marry him.

Once the award had been conferred, the wise fool was asked what his plans were for the future.

'I'm hoping to get the world title next,' he said.

'You mean, to be the Stupidest Man in the World?'

Nasrudin shook his head.

'Yes.'

'D'you think you have a chance at realizing your dream?' the official asked.

Nasrudin squawked like a chicken.

'Pink red red red yellow blue!'

'Is that your answer?'

'Bottle coat handbag ferret!'

'Why are you talking jibberish all of a sudden?'

'Because I just remembered something.'

'What?'

'If I answer your questions properly, I wouldn't be so stupid as to have a chance at winning the title for the Stupidest Man in the World.'

ANKARA
TURKEY

A Question of Taste

During his travels, Nasrudin was befriended by an ordinary-looking local who seemed to thrive on the stranger's back-to-front way of seeing things.

As the days passed, the wise fool came to understand the local was in fact a billionaire, with properties and businesses all over the world. Not wishing to offend his new friend, Nasrudin pretended that he liked the very same things as him. The tycoon, who was used to people sidling up in search of money, asked if the traveller was pretending to like the things he did.

Fearful at being rumbled and losing the friendship, Nasrudin winced.

'My taste is impartial,' he replied awkwardly. 'Indeed, it's so impartial it has a will of its own.'

LEERDAM
THE NETHERLANDS

The Warner

While on his peregrinations through the Netherlands, Nasrudin spotted a row of steel wind turbines on the horizon.

Terrified out of his wits, he assumed they were an army of ogres approaching.

The wise fool rushed through the streets of the nearest village he came to, screaming for people to protect themselves from the invading force.

Contrary to what he expected, the villagers threw pots and pans at him from their windows.

Begging the people to listen to him, he flailed his arms around, doing his best to act out the motion of the invading ogres.

But the villagers just hurled more pots and pans in his direction.

'What a strange land this is,' Nasrudin said to himself. 'The people are not fearful of invading ogres, but they're apparently terrified of the man who warns them of such creatures!'

MADRE DE DIOS
PERU

Lost City Found

Nasrudin had searched for 'Paititi', the great lost city of the Incas, for months in the cloud forest.

The journey had reduced him and his team to madness, and to an array of terrible illnesses, including malaria and dengue fever.

One morning, scaling a rock face in deep jungle, the wise fool discovered the ruined city that had eluded adventurers for centuries.

Cheers rang out over the canopy of trees below.

Once measurements and photographs had been taken, Nasrudin gave the order to leave the ruins behind and to delete the grid coordinates from their equipment.

The team of adventurers and porters regarded their leader in horror.

'Why do you want to leave?' one of the porters asked in stupefaction. 'After all, we have risked our lives many times over to locate the lost city.'

Nasrudin sighed.

'If we don't tiptoe away and pretend we never found it,' he replied, 'we'd be preventing other explorers from having all the fun we ourselves have had!'

AARAU

SWITZERLAND

Trapping Time

asrudin went on eBay and spent all his money on cuckoo clocks.

When they arrived, he locked them in his cupboard.

'What are you doing?' his friend asked.

'Trapping time.'

'That's not how it works. Clocks are not time, they merely register time.'

'I have every confidence that, in their ardent desire to be freed,' said Nasrudin, 'they'll go and tell time that they're trapped.'

LAGOS
NIGERIA

Fish Taste

Nasrudin had been appointed Professor of Natural Sciences at the University of Lagos.

On the first day of lecturing, a student asked him if water had a taste.

'Yes it does,' the wise fool responded. 'But nature has programmed us not to notice it, so we're aware when the taste has been adulterated or flavoured.'

Persistent by nature, the student posed a second question:

'How could you know such things?' she asked. 'After all, we supposedly experience the sense of taste in the same way.'

'I know this,' the professor retorted, 'because three years ago I had fish tastebuds implanted in my mouth.'

'Does that mean you taste things as a fish does?'

'Yes it does.'

'And how does water taste to you?'

'Like swimming-pool water does to you,' said Nasrudin.

FLORENCE
ITALY

North Dark

As an enthusiastic student of the Old Masters, Nasrudin saved up to take an exclusive painting course in Florence.

He chose the course because it claimed to recreate the exact conditions used by the likes of Michelangelo, Da Vinci, and Raphael. The same kinds of canvas, paints, brushes, and even light were used.

On the first day, the students were not even permitted to pick up a brush. Rather, they were expected to consider light.

And, in particular, north light.

Less direct, and therefore more constant, north light – as it was explained – was optimum, and ought therefore to be used always.

On the second day, the students were reminded that north light was what they would have to use if they wanted to recreate the magic of the Old Masters. So as to prove they understood this, the class was asked to draw an image by the next day.

All afternoon, Nasrudin struggled to decide what he would paint.

At first, he decided to do a study of a little jar of flowers. But then he saw a marble bust in the corner of the studio and made up his mind to paint it.

A few minutes later, he forgot about the bust and decided to paint the actual brushes he was working with.

Hours of indecision slipped by.

At midnight he was still deliberating.

Next morning, the professor asked each of the students to show the work they'd painted in north light.

When it came to Nasrudin, he pulled a sheet from his easel, revealing a monstrous clutter of jagged lines.

'What on earth is that?!' the instructor growled.

'Unfortunately, all the north light ran out,' the wise fool answered obsequiously, 'so I was forced to use north dark instead.'

AMMAN
JORDAN

Old Lamps for New

Nasrudin was found exchanging old brass lamps for new ones from a ramshackle cart in the market.

Another stallholder asked as a joke if he was behaving like the evil merchant in the story of Aladdin from *A Thousand and One Nights*.

'You never know…' he answered. 'Just as I am playing the role of Aladdin from the story, perhaps there's a jinn out there who's playing the part of the jinn – and is hiding in one of the battered old lamps!'

KHARTOUM
SUDAN

Incompatible Friends

Nasrudin had a pet scorpion called Wilbur that he'd bought from a dealer deep in the bazaar.

The two were inseparable and would spend the long hot days together. The wise fool would recount tales of his adventures to the little jet-black arachnid and would feed him dainty morsels of meat.

People would always ask whether there was a danger of being stung.

'Wilbur's like a son to me!' Nasrudin would exclaim. 'He loves me, and I love him!'

Months passed, in which the friendship between man and scorpion grew all the stronger.

But then, one day, Wilbur flicked his tail down in a moment of high excitement and stung his owner badly on the hand.

As he felt the poison entering his bloodstream, Nasrudin looked at his pet in bewilderment.

'My dearest friend, it may have been nothing more than a little love bite to you,' he gasped, 'but to me, it's likely to be a matter of life and death!'

MUNICH
GERMANY

The Cello Hunter

Nasrudin heard that, for two centuries, the rarest of all Stradivarius cellos had been lost.

He was dead set on finding it.

Setting out on a grand adventure on the quest for the missing instrument, he scoured much of the known world for more than thirty years. Despite having plenty of leads, he never managed to find the prized instrument.

Three decades after embarking on the quest, someone asked the wise fool why he'd been so unlucky.

'Unlucky?' he snapped. 'Are you mad? The search for the lost Stradivarius has given a purpose to my life and has provided me with adventure in huge measure. Had I not searched for that fabled cello, I'd have stayed in my village and done nothing at all.'

'But aren't you forlorn at not finding it?'

'Of course not,' Nasrudin rejoined.

'Why not?'

'Because the hunt was always going to be sweeter than the capture of the beast.'

TUCSON
ARIZONA

Recognition

Nasrudin had read an article in a copy of the *National Inquirer* that an asteroid was about to hit Earth and would kill off 99% of the world's population.

Terrified out of his wits, he hurried to a cryonic suspension laboratory in Tucson, Arizona, where bodies were preserved in liquid nitrogen to be resurrected in the future.

After filling out a comprehensive questionnaire, the wise fool was given an interview, then asked if he had any questions.

'Is it possible for me to be frozen with my donkey?' he asked.

The representative of the cryonics company winced.

'I suppose it's possible for an additional fee,' he said. 'But may I enquire why you would want to have the animal frozen with you?'

'Well, after the asteroid strike,' Nasrudin explained, 'it's likely that all my friends and family will be dead.'

'So you are worried there will be no one to look after your donkey?'

The wise fool shook his head.

'No, not that.'

'Then?'

'If everyone I know is gone, how will there be anyone to tell me who I am once I thaw out?' Nasrudin said. 'With no one else but me able to recognize the donkey, it's vital that I'm there, too, to inform her that she is who she is.'

ASHKHABAD
TURKMENISTAN

Magic Bag

Although not usually tempted to part with his hard-scrounged funds, the wise fool noticed a curious velvet bag in the bazaar of Ashkhabad.

The size of a pillowcase, the object had been fashioned expertly, its surface festooned with cryptic symbols.

'How much is that old bag?' he asked.

The stall-keeper grunted a low price, and Nasrudin passed over a coin.

That night, in the guesthouse where he was staying, he took a closer look at the bag. But as he reached for it, he thought of the apple cake that his mother used to make.

To his amazement, he smelled the very same cake.

Sticking his hand into the bag, he found that it was inside, waiting for him to pull it out and feast.

Pinching himself to make sure he wasn't having one of his daydreams, the wise fool concluded that he was not dreaming and that, by some quirk of fate and fortune, he had purchased a magic bag.

Having gobbled up the apple cake, he thought of a bar of solid gold.

Slipping his hand into the bag, he found the ingot inside.

Next, he imagined a gold Rolex watch, a new silk shirt, and a new saddle for his donkey.

As soon as the objects were thought of, they appeared. Even more remarkable was that the bag seemed to expand to produce objects that would normally have been too large to be contained inside.

All night, Nasrudin thought of objects.

One by one, they appeared.

He even thought of the magic bag, and another one – exactly the same – appeared.

By dawn, the wise fool was sitting amid piles of loot – from cages filled with exotic birds, to rare treasures found in distant lands, to sacks of gems, to laptop computers, iPhones, and exquisite clothing fit for a king.

Yawning, he was about to go to bed when, for no reason at all, he thought of himself sitting there – surrounded by loot.

A moment later, a perfect clone of himself stepped out of the bag.

'Hello,' he said, 'I'm Nasrudin.'

Furious at having been cloned, the wise fool grabbed the bag and reprimanded it.

'I am your master, not this imposter! If you dare forget it, I'll take you to the ocean and hurl you over the cliff!'

At that moment, there was a blinding flash.

The ocean, and the cliff high above, were conjured into existence.

As for the wise fool, his home, and all his new loot, were never seen again.

AGASSIZ ICE CAP
ARCTIC

The Polar Bear

Nasrudin's digestive tract was gripped by a wild rumpus of motion and commotion.

It was soon clear that swallowing a snow leopard cub hadn't solved anything at all.

While taking refuge in a smoke-filled yurt on a hillside far from anywhere, the wise fool learned his destiny from a shaman.

'You must go to the white cap of the planet, and talk to the white bear,' she said.

'The white cap…? You mean the polar ice cap?'

The shaman nodded.

'And by the white bear, you mean a polar bear?'

The shaman smiled.

'You must leave at once,' she said.

Clambering to his feet, Nasrudin left the yurt behind him and trudged across one horizon after the next until he reached Ulaanbaatar.

After a gruelling journey, he came to an expanse of Arctic tundra, the likes of which he'd never imagined existed.

Stooped low in the distance was a polar bear, its nose ranged high and to the side, as the creature caught the scent of an intruder.

Groaning at the sacrifices he'd made in the name of a cure, and cursing the bluebottle that had caused all the trouble in the first place, the wise fool lay down on his stomach and opened his mouth.

Curious at what kind of creature the intruder might be, the polar bear paced forward at double speed.

Less than a minute later, the creature was inside Nasrudin's stomach.

'Gotcha!' the troubled trailblazer exclaimed. 'That'll teach you – you damned snow leopard!'

OXFORD

ENGLAND

Making Haste

Nasrudin was seen rushing down the street.

A friend called out asking what the haste was all about.

'I've got to catch up with myself!' the wise fool yelled. 'You see, I went out to buy milk, and then realized that I already have some at home. So I have to catch myself before I buy any more!'

KONYA
TURKEY

Heaven and Earth

asrudin had just visited the tomb of the revered Sufi Jalaluddin Rumi, and had discovered a shaded café in a square.

Sitting down, he ordered a cup of coffee.

At the next table, two elderly men were arguing loudly.

'They come here every day,' the waiter whispered to Nasrudin as he served him, 'and every day they go at one another like this. It's been going on for years!'

'What do they argue about?' Nasrudin asked.

'Listen to them and you'll hear for yourself.'

So, being a visitor with an interest in local culture, Nasrudin leaned towards the arguing men and listened.

The first man insisted the sky above was an illusion, but that the ground beneath the table was real.

The second argued the opposite was true – that the ground was an illusion and the sky was real.

Realizing that Nasrudin was listening in, the men suggested that he decide which of them was right.

'If I were to pass judgment,' he said, 'one of you would surely be pleased, and the other displeased.'

'That is so,' the first man said.

'But at least we would have an answer,' the other chimed in.

'Let's meet here tomorrow,' the wise fool said. 'By then I would have had a night to sleep on it.'

It was agreed, and the next day all three men met again at the same café.

'Have you decided which one of us is right?' the first man asked.

Nasrudin swallowed hard.

'I thought about nothing else,' he answered, 'but I haven't come up with a decision. So, I suggest we meet again at the same time tomorrow.'

Again it was agreed, and again the three men met the following afternoon.

'Have you reached a decision on which of us is right?' the second man asked.

'Not quite yet,' Nasrudin replied. 'You see, this is a very difficult judgment to make. I'll need another night.'

The following day, the three men met once again, then on the fourth day, the fifth, and the sixth.

At the end of a week, the arguing men had lost their patience.

'It's time to decide!' the first man snapped.

'If you don't make a decision right now,' the other said, toying with a knife, 'you'll regret it!'

The wise fool took a sip of his coffee, sighed heavily, and pulled a coin from his pocket. As the arguing men watched, he threw it high into the air. A bird that was flapping by snatched it in its beak and flew away.

Nasrudin took out a second coin, and dropped it on the ground beneath the table. In reaching down for it, his fingers covered it in dirt.

The arguing men looked at one another, then at Nasrudin.

'Which one of us is right and which is wrong?' they demanded.

'As you saw for yourselves,' the wise fool said, 'the coin vanished when thrown into the sky, which surely proves the sky does not exist. And when a coin was tossed onto the ground, it vanished, too… so the ground doesn't exist either.'

'Then which of us is right?' the first man growled.

'You're both right,' Nasrudin said. 'Then, again, you're both wrong.'

'How can we be right *and* wrong at the same time?' the second man hissed.

The wise fool got to his feet.

'The score you asked me to settle is over,' he said. 'I suggest you fight this one out among yourselves.'

DISNEYLAND
PARIS

Speak, Not Hear

Nasrudin got a job at Disneyland and was given a Donald Duck costume to wear.

On the first day, he was sent out to amuse the children.

Spotting a little girl in a floral print dress, the wise fool was overcome with greed for the ice cream she was eating.

So, still dressed as Donald Duck, he marched up to the girl and grabbed the ice cream.

Almost instantly a supervisor marched over and reprimanded the errant worker.

'Do anything like that again,' he roared, 'and I'll see that you're fired right away!'

Nasrudin shrugged.

'I'm sorry, I'm a duck and so I don't understand what you're saying.'

'But you're speaking to me in English!' the Disneyland official hollered back.

'I may be speaking it,' Nasrudin retorted, 'but that doesn't mean I understand it when others speak it to me!'

DUBLIN

IRELAND

School for Back-to-Front Thinking

aving been an outcast for far too long, Nasrudin decided it was time he made something of himself.

So he thought and he thought, and came up with a plan.

He would start the first School for Back-to-Front Thinking and teach others to observe the world around them as he did.

Scrounging money from anyone stupid enough to lend it, and doing much of the construction himself, he put up a headquarters in the middle of the Irish capital.

Then, amid much fanfare, he mounted a social media campaign to announce the opening of the School for Back-to-Front Thinking.

On the first day, Nasrudin entered his building by the special door reserved for staff, and waited.

But, despite widespread interest, no one turned up.

That evening, the wise fool was spotted by a friend sitting on a park bench, looking forlorn.

'How did the big launch go?' he asked brightly.

'A total disaster.'

'Why? After all, you got masses of media attention.'

'I don't know. I just don't understand it.'

The friend asked whether he could see the school, and the two walked the short distance to the building.

'Come in through the staff entrance,' Nasrudin said.

Taking in the school's imposing exterior, the friend paused.

'Why aren't there any windows or doors?' he asked.

'Because I was saving money. And doors and windows are far too expensive. So I did away with them.'

'Where's the door?'

'Here. This is it.'

'But it's marked "staff entrance".'

'Yes, it's for staff.'

'Can students use it?'

'Of course not!' the wise fool riposted angrily.

'So… tell me… how were your students meant to get inside?'

Nasrudin exhaled.

'That was going to be the first lesson I taught them,' he said.

MAZAR-I-SHARIF
AFGHANISTAN

Father and Son

The son of the wise fool excelled in video games, and everything else relating to technology leaving his father far behind.

Rather than being pleased at the skill of the up-and-coming generation, Nasrudin was bitter.

'He's better than me in absolutely everything,' he moaned to a friend in the teahouse. 'I look at things which, until recently, I was better at... and marvel that he's surpassed me even though he's so young.'

'You wait,' the friend chipped in, 'it'll only get worse as he gets older.'

A look of fear descended over Nasrudin's face.

'Well, I hope I always stay older than my son,' he whimpered, 'but I suppose with time he'll beat me on that as well.'

Finis

THE MISADVENTURES OF THE MYSTIFYING NASRUDIN

TAHIR SHAH

THE VOYAGES AND VICISSITUDES OF NASRUDIN

TAHIR SHAH

TRAVELS WITH NASRUDIN

TAHIR SHAH

A REQUEST

If you enjoyed this book, please review it on your favourite online retailer or review website.

Reviews are an author's best friend.

To stay in touch with Tahir Shah, and to hear about his upcoming releases before anyone else, please sign up for his mailing list:

 http://tahirshah.com/newsletter

And to follow him on social media, please go to any of the following links:

 http://www.twitter.com/humanstew

 @tahirshah999

 http://www.facebook.com/TahirShahAuthor

 http://www.youtube.com/user/tahirshah999

 http://www.pinterest.com/tahirshah

 https://www.goodreads.com/tahirshahauthor

http://www.tahirshah.com